JESSICA'S SEARCH

The Secret of Ballycater Cove

JESSICA'S SEARCH

The Secret of Ballycater Cove

ADRIAN ROBERT GOSTICK

DESERET BOOK COMPANY
SALT LAKE CITY, UTAH

Library of Congress Cataloging-in-Publication Data
  Gostick, Adrian Robert.
    Jessica's search : the secret of Ballycater Cove / Adrian Robert
  Gostick.
      p.   cm.
    Summary: The arrival of two missionaries in her Newfoundland
  fishing village leads sixteen-year-old Jessica to rediscover her
  lost faith in the Mormon Church, as she tries to deal with her
  father's disappearance at sea.
    ISBN 1-57345-436-2
    [1. Death—Fiction. 2. Mormons—Fiction. 3. Missionaries—
  Fiction. 4. Newfoundland—Fiction. 5. Canada—Fiction.]
  I. Title.
  PZ7.G6924Je   1998
  [Fic.]—dc21   98-34567
                                            CIP
                                            AC

Printed in the United States of America   21239 - 6423

10 9 8 7 6 5 4 3 2

For Jennifer and Tony

1

SEPTEMBER 17, 1856

There was a moment of complete silence on the water, which was rare. The voices of the men on the fishing boat dropped away to nothing; ropes hung from calloused hands as they watched the fog roll toward them. Then in a rush they began frantically to work—turning the boat and pulling in the nets that were holding the small ship down like weights.

Less than a minute passed before a man shouted from the crow's nest, "It's on us!" and they all turned and stared toward the shore . . . or where the shore should have been . . . and realized the fog had filled the cove and had caught them with their nets still heavy in the water. The cold, gray mist slithered over the deck and mounted the mainsail like a white snake.

Adam Blake, the youngest of the *Ballycater's* crew, stood paralyzed, his face deathbed pale. He watched the men run frantically from one end of the boat to the other, but he didn't help them. He couldn't move.

"I've got fifteen yards off starboard," yelled Adam's brother, waving his hands in the air in frustration. Adam broke from his trance and ran to his brother's side.

"It won't come in?" Adam asked.

"No. Help me pull," said his brother, and they strained to drag the fifteen yards of heavy, wet netting into the boat.

"No, cut it!" yelled the captain.

His brother unsheathed his knife and cut the valuable net strand by strand. Finally, the last lead rope was cut and the heavy net fell into the ocean with a splash. They didn't see it hit the water; the fog was too thick.

"It's free," he yelled at the captain.

"Grab an oar," the captain yelled back.

The boat began moving slowly, blindly in the fog.

"Open sea is out there . . . somewhere," his brother rasped.

Adam was about to answer when the *Ballycater* rose on a fierce wave and tilted at an awkward angle. The men lunged to find a foothold, but sliding down the swell, the boat twisted back violently and smashed against something under the water. The wood of the hull groaned and then gave way with an earsplitting snap. Within seconds the deck was awash in salt water, which just as quickly poured back over the side as the boat rose sharply on the next wave.

"We're going down," said a deep voice from aft.

"Adam!" It was his brother's voice, searching for him. They'd become separated and the fog was thicker— frustratingly white.

Adam ran until his legs hit the rail on the port side and then he raced back to starboard. He screamed for his brother, but by then there were too many voices yelling in the mist. Finally he collapsed on his knees on the wet deck.

He had given up when he felt himself being lifted and tossed without a word overboard. He fell head over heels through the damp air and hit the icy water feet first.

My great grandfather, Adam Blake, was the only survivor of the sinking of the *Ballycater*.

2

TODAY

After the night's rain the sandy beach was spongy and soft under my feet. I took my time—placing each foot carefully and then lifting it high and clear to make sure I left a perfect imprint with every step. When I reached the ocean I smiled to myself and, without turning, began retracing my footsteps. It only took me a few minutes to reach the steps in the rock wall. Then I jumped out of the sand and stood on the first step admiring the set of one-way footprints into the surf.

It was still early and hardly anyone else was awake, only the fishermen loading their nets along the pier. In the distance I could hear the first of their diesel engines fire up. She'd be waking up soon. I raced up the stone steps and leaned against the metal rail at the top of the wall, practicing my most casual pose. A minute or two passed, and I couldn't wait any longer. I shot off up the road, passed Chern's store, and sprinted up Shoreline Drive to her house. I banged heavily on the back door and waited.

"What?" Jessica asked, sticking her head out of her second-story bedroom window.

I leaned back on my heels and looked up. "It's clear,"

I said, waving an arm in the air. "Thought you might want to take a spin around the bay in my new boat."

She scowled and looked to the ocean. "Ah, it'll probably rain and sink that little dingy of yours."

My shoulders slumped, but then I saw a sly curl at the corner of her mouth and I laughed. "Come on, or I'll take my *other* best friend."

In a few minutes Jessica appeared at the back door, wearing her favorite, ratty v-neck sweater and baseball cap, and we walked back along Shoreline. When we neared Chern's store I grabbed her baseball cap, and she chased me up Chern's porch and down his front steps to the metal railing of the quay, the rock wall that lines the beach. I slowed just a step and she grabbed me by the waist and I let her pull me to a stop.

"Wow, look at that," I said, pointing over the rock and down to the sand below.

"What?"

"Those footsteps. They just go out to sea. That's spooky."

She studied them for a time, then wrinkled her nose. "It's just . . ." she hesitated. It *was* weird.

We walked slowly down the rock steps and stood beside the fresh footprints.

"You think we should report this?" I asked.

Jessica didn't answer. A cool wind blew off the ocean and we both shivered.

"I bet I know what this is," I said quietly, as mysteriously as possible. "It's the ghost of some drowned fisherman from the *Ballycater* who came back to find his long lost family. Maybe he came back . . . farther up the beach . . . but his family wouldn't let him in 'cause he wasn't all there. . . . I bet parts of him had been eaten by fish. . . ."

Jessica bent down to examine the footprints.

" . . . but he still wants to find his family. So he'll be back. There he is!" I shouted, grabbing Jessica by the arm.

She stood up. "Real scary, Ian," she said, rolling her eyes and then kicking sand over my boots. "And this headless fisherman from the nineteenth century just happens to wear big old Nike hiking boots like yours?" she asked.

"They were very popular back then."

She laughed and ran lightly down the footprints to the water's edge. "You did a very good job. Almost no mistakes. I'm proud of you."

"Aw, it was a ghost from the *Ballycater*," I said, running heavily to catch up.

We turned when we reached the water and walked slowly along the sand. As we walked, Jessica picked up seashells and tossed them back into the surf while my mind carefully built the first question of the day.

By most accounts, I'm a pretty normal sixteen-year-old. I'm tall and square, mostly muscle and sinew. My mom cuts my hair and it usually sticks up in funny directions, but Jessica's told me I'm handsome enough. She's even said that when we go to town, the girls in Basques look at me and giggle. I guess my only abnormality is my curiosity. I don't know why I'm so curious. I've lived my entire life in Wolf Point, an isolated Newfoundland outport. Only three hundred people live here, and yet I'm actually interested in all of them, but perhaps in Jessica more than anyone. At one time or another I've asked her every question imaginable, but I can still find new things to ask.

"If you could go back in time, what would you want to invent?" I asked as we walked along the beach.

5

She shook her head. "You asked me that last week, Ian."

"Did not."

"Yes you did. Or maybe it was last month. But you've asked me that before."

I thought harder.

"Okay, if you were stuck on a deserted island with just one person, who would you want it to be?"

"And I'm supposed to say you, right?"

"No, that's too easy. You can't say me."

"My dad."

"You can't say him, either. Pick someone famous."

"William Shakespeare."

"He's dead. He wouldn't be much fun."

She laughed. "I don't know, who would you—"

Her voice was lost as in the distance another fisherman's diesel engine roared to life. Jessica checked her watch and smiled. "I bet that's Dad. We could tag along, if you want."

I shrugged. I had really wanted to take my new boat out on the water, and for some reason the thought of sharing Jessica for the day brought on a pang of jealousy. I didn't know where the feeling came from. We're just friends. I do not—absolutely do not—have romantic feelings for her.

It isn't that she's ugly. Jessica is sort of attractive, I guess. In fact, on Saturday nights, when she puts on makeup, she looks kind of cute if I squint a bit. But she definitely is not dating material. She is just one of the guys. Any-way, she's too skinny and her hair isn't poofy and soft like the girls' in Basques. Jessica always wears it pulled back in a ponytail, so it doesn't fly in her face when she rides a bike or is out on the water. She does have nice eyes, though, but she complains that they're too big for her face. She also says her laugh is too girlish. But she's okay, I've reasoned on more than one occasion. But she is not kissable. Yuck.

I shook off the jealousy. "Yeah, I guess. Whatever."

"Come on, then." She raced back up the beach and took the stone steps two at a time. I followed, and we ran together along the wooden wharf until the pier opened up before us. Her dad's boat was still in its mooring, puffing black smoke out of its tall exhaust pipe. He was just about to cast off when we sprinted up, panting.

"We . . . wanna . . . go," she said between breaths.

Her dad looked at her and frowned. "Um, I don't know . . . I guess not. Not today. Sorry."

She laughed and took a step to climb aboard. He was always kidding.

"I'm serious, Jessica," he said.

Her face went serious. "Why not?"

"Because I don't know where I'm heading today, and I don't want to be watching you."

"You don't have to watch us. We're not babies."

"All the same."

She folded her arms and then smiled again. "He'll let us. Just come on." She jumped off the pier and landed in the trawler.

Her father calmly stepped to the helm and shut the engine down. It died with an awkward *splunk,* and the last black plume of exhaust lifted itself into the morning sky. I stood on the pier, not about to follow Jessica's lead. Her father walked over and stood within inches of her face. They were almost the same height, but her dad was built like a wrestler and was an imposing figure.

7

"I've asked you nicely," he said. "Now I'm telling you. No. Not today."

Jessica's grin disappeared and turned into a wide scowl. "Fine. You never take me anymore."

"That's not true."

"Just go then." With that she jumped out of the boat, folded her arms, and strode back down the pier.

"Bye," I said, without looking directly at Jess's dad. "Have a safe day."

"Thanks, Ian," he said.

Her father fired the engine back up, and I helped him cast off. For a while, I stood and watched as her father's boat steamed out. The boat rode high in the water, and its stern left a thick wake in the ocean. Her dad was alone on the bridge, looking out to sea. He had one hand on the wheel and the other on his hip, like an explorer.

Eventually Jessica reappeared and we walked to the outer end of the pier and stood there until the boat took a turn around the channel buoy near the far north shore and disappeared into the distance. It was windy, as always, but the horizon was clear. We lived in a fishing village—we always checked the horizon.

"So you wanna take a ride now?" I asked.

She didn't answer for a moment then shook her head. "I guess not. I don't really feel like it anymore."

"I'd go," said a girl's voice. I spun around, but the pier was deserted. I heard the girl laughing. Her voice was coming from under the pier.

"It's Megan," I realized, catching a glimpse of my little sister through a space between the planks. "She's under the pier again, spying."

Jessica smiled and dropped to her hands and knees

and peered between the wooden boards. "I seeee you," she said.

Megan squealed and jumped between the cross beams.

"I'm gonna spit on her," I said.

"Don't you dare," said Jessica. "Be careful under there, Megan. You could fall into the water."

"She can swim," I added, helpfully. "Anyway, my mom told her to stop listening in on people's conversations. Especially mine." I tried to think if I'd said anything embarrassing in the past few minutes, but couldn't remember.

"You guys wanna do something?" Megan asked from below.

Jessica smiled. "No thanks. I think I'm gonna head home for awhile. I got into a fight with my dad."

"I heard."

"You shouldn't have," I said.

"It's all right," said Jessica.

* * * * *

We didn't take a boat ride that day.

Eventually, Jessica walked back home and spent the day inside, out of the wind, probably reading and listening to the radio. It was just a regular boring day . . . until night fell and her father hadn't come home.

3

THE SEA

Jessica's dad was a terrible singer. Once, when everyone was singing Christmas carols at a town party, Jessica had leaned over and asked if he could sing a little quieter, maybe even just mouth the words to the song. She'd said that his voice was making all the people around him go off key. Common sense told him she was right, but the criticism still stung.

So he saved his singing for the ocean, where there was no one to hear except the occasional seagull. He spent his days making up songs as he let his fishing nets out or hauled in his heavy catch. He never told anyone that he sang while he worked, and chances are Jessica would have tormented him mercilessly if he had. But it was one of his simple joys in life. And that morning, under a huge clear blue sky, he sang loudly as he worked. Mostly, he sang to forget the morning fight with his daughter.

> *Colin was a fisherman*
> *There wasn't any finer man*
> *To Newfoundland they sent him*
> *But they said he'd never pull 'em in*

He paused for a minute, smiling to himself as he untangled a lead rope and made up more lyrics, then plowed on:

He showed them all they was wrong
When he caught a hundred like a song
They'd never seen the like before
But the next day he caught some more

Before noon he had already pulled in a good day's haul, and the deck of his boat was buried under a thick silver blanket of fish. It had been months, maybe years since he'd had a morning like this, and as he worked he figured the tonnage and price, subtracted gasoline, and estimated he was ankle-deep in several hundred dollars worth of Atlantic cod.

He scratched the boat along the green hull—like it was a horse—and whispered, "Keep up the good work, old girl. I'll give you a sugar cube if you get us another ton."

He looked over the side. The sea was beginning to churn, picking his little boat up without effort, but he couldn't quit yet. He began restringing net along the trawler's port arm, then lowered the arm and dropped the heavy mesh into the sea. The weights dragged the net underwater and he turned to start the engine. Then he felt it.

He knew the feeling well; he'd had it before many times. It started deep in his chest and spread quickly to his arms and legs. It made it hard to breathe. It was as if a small voice had whispered to him of something ominous out on the water.

"That's the Spirit talking," his wife told him on more than one occasion. She was a Mormon and believed in that kind of thing.

12

"Ahhh. No spirit would come near me. I'm too cantankerous," he'd reply. He didn't have any interest in religion. For him, the feeling was a sailor's sixth sense, nothing more.

He scanned the horizon and realized only then that he'd drifted close to the foggy shore and that the waves were too high for comfort. Still, his net was in the water and pulling it in without a catch would be the waste of a precious hour of daylight. He looked over the horizon once more and decided to take one last pass through the cove and then head out to sea.

The wave caught him only minutes later.

It had built without warning around the ragged north edge of the cove and was rolling like a barrel toward his trawler. Jessica's father was leaning over the side when he heard a hiss that made his heart race. Out of the corner of his eye he saw a dark shadow moving. He didn't need to turn; thirty years at sea had taught him what was coming. He pulled his boots with a *suck* out of the layer of fish on the deck and lunged for the wheel. Spinning it frantically, he tried to swing the trawler around to face the monstrous wave racing toward him across the cove.

By the time the wall of water reached him, it was as tall as the mast and about to break. He held on to the wheel and fought to keep his balance as the little craft rode up the wave, tilting crazily, hanging at an impossible angle. As the trawler reached the breaking crest, he was wrenched away from the wheel and thrown to the deck. The fisherman reached for the railing, but before he could grab hold, the tiny boat was hurled back down the face of the wave as lightly as if it were one of those Viking ships in a carnival ride.

* * * * *

He awoke in the ocean.

He heard splashing first. It took a second for his mind to clear, and at first he thought a whale was lying on his chest. But then he opened his eyes and realized he was pinned under a corner of his overturned trawler and that he was breathing an unnatural mixture of salt water and air. His legs and body were snarled in nets and rigging, and under the immense weight of the rocking boat he had to kick frantically to keep his head out of the icy water. As the boat dipped before rising on a wave, there was just enough time to gasp for air.

For what seemed like an hour he fought to keep his head above water, but each minute of struggle brought the ropes and net more tightly around his legs. His mind kept flashing to Jessica, first to the fight they'd had that morning and then back to scenes from her childhood. He remembered the school program when she was fourteen, when she had played the fiddle and another boy had played the bagpipes and despite the mistakes the music was haunting and beautiful. She hadn't played for a few years. When he got out of this mess he would ask her why. Then she was four, and he was reading her a bedtime story in her attic room. As he kissed her goodnight he'd asked, "How much do you love me?" and she'd answered, "Fifty pounds of fish in your ear, that's how much." He had laughed and kissed her again, and remembering, he smiled.

Another hour passed and his strength was gone. The water was ice cold and now the waves were dropping and the boat was slowing to a steady rock, giving him less opportunity to breathe. He gasped, but took in only a mouthful of sea water. He coughed and strained with all

14

his force against the ropes that held him captive. He couldn't die now. He hadn't said good-bye to his wife, to his daughter.

Then, with a last frantic bid to live, he lunged at a rope hanging over the side.

4

MISSING

Sometime after midnight the phone rang at my house. I stayed under the covers, but listened to the muffled sound of my dad's voice. The phone was hung up and there were a few quiet words between my parents as slickers and boots were collected. Then the door to the outside closed and dad was gone.

I crawled out of bed and went into their room. Mom was sitting up in bed, staring at her palm.

"What is it?" I asked.

She looked up, surprised. "Oh, Ian," she said, then looked down.

"What is it?" I asked again.

She took a breath, "It was Jessica's mom."

"And?"

"It's Colin, her dad. . . . He hasn't come back."

My mouth dropped open. "I'm going with Dad."

That woke her up and she pointed her finger. "No. You stay put."

I threw my arms in the air and stormed around the room.

"No," she said, before I could open my mouth again.

I stomped over to the window and pulled the curtain

aside. Outside I could see a few dark houses, yellow and pale-blue in the moonlight with windows that looked like eyes. Above, the sky was full of stars—a good night to be out on the water. I walked through the house and eventually pulled on my coat and went out onto the porch where I stuck my hands deep in my pockets. Nights on The Rock are always cold and damp, even in late summer, and I could see my breath.

I thought about Jess's dad: that I was the last person to speak to him before he left, that I really didn't know much about him. Her dad was quiet. He had arms like cables, thick and strong from pulling nets since he was a kid. He'd taken Jess and I fishing a few times. Once, before I had even turned ten, Mr. O'Brien had let me steer his boat on the open water. He let me steer for more than an hour, until I got tired.

But that's all I knew about him. Then I thought about Jess.

She probably wasn't crying. I'd never seen her cry, and I wondered if anything could make her cry. She was as tough as any Newfie. Once, she'd fallen through one of the slats on the pier and ripped her leg so bad she needed fifteen stitches. When I had tried to help she pushed me away and pulled her leg out by herself. Then we walked up to the store. She didn't cry; she didn't even run. She just walked, with blood oozing out everywhere, as though nothing had happened, and talked about how she'd never had a scar before.

I sat down hard on the porch swing and suddenly realized I was jealous again. Not a romantic kind of jealous, I told myself, just the kind that you get when you've been best friends since you can walk and you expect the other person to call you when there's a problem, to need

17

you. But, I thought, *Jess doesn't need anyone.* She's always been that way.

* * * * *

Jessica Lanny McDonald O'Brien had been born in Newfoundland.

In 1982, just before she was born, her family moved to Wolf Point, Newfoundland, and bought the old house overlooking the harbor—next door to us.

Where we live is a small fishing "outport," located on a remote part of Canada's eastern-most island near Channel-Port-aux-Basques. It's fifty-five minutes by boat to the nearest mall or movie theater, longer if the waves are up. The Rock, as locals call Newfoundland, is cold and wet all the time. It's so cold that at night, before your body has a chance to warm them, the sheets on your bed are as slick as ice. So cold that most of us have always left our front doors unlocked, because keys break off in the frozen locks. So cold . . . well, you get the idea.

My family, the Blakes, have always been here. The first Blakes came to The Rock more than 200 years ago. But Jessica's family were relative newcomers. And most of us thought they were probably the strangest people on the island.

For example, there was the matter of Jess's name— Jessica Lanny McDonald O'Brien.

The spring Jess was born, the Toronto Maple Leafs were in the Stanley Cup playoffs following what had been a pretty good season—led that year by the playmaking of defenseman Borje Salming, the stingy goaltending of Mike Palmateer, and the deft scoring touch of rightwinger Lanny McDonald.

Mr. O'Brien was a big Maple Leafs fan. In fact, while his wife was delivering in the hospital in Basques,

18

Mr. O'Brien watched Game 7 of the quarterfinals on TV in the waiting room. By the time the doctor came out to say his wife was about ready to deliver the baby, the Maple Leafs and the Montreal Canadiens—the Habs—were locked in a scoreless overtime battle.

Since he liked a good game of hockey as much as the next Newfie, the doctor stayed. And finally, when the CBC announcer screamed in a breathless frenzy that Lanny McDonald had scored and the Leafs would advance to the semifinals, both the doctor and Mr. O'Brien had the same idea: the kid's name must be Lanny McDonald O'Brien.

But an hour later, when a little girl was born, the men didn't know what to do. Thinking quickly, they named the girl Jessica Lanny McDonald O'Brien before Mrs. O'Brien had a chance to slap them both.

Mr. O'Brien never got a hockey-playing son, so Jess grew up in that boy's place.

In fact, the two of us grew up as much brothers as friends. For the past sixteen years we've spent part of most every day together, and much of the time has been spent getting into trouble. When we were seven, we set Mrs. Scott's cat adrift on some driftwood, and Jess's dad had to take out a boat and rescue the thing before it got caught in the riptide. When we were nine we climbed up on my roof to watch the sunset, but discovered a loose shingle. Jess tried to fix it, but ended up pulling it out. It left a nasty hole, and I reasoned: "Maybe if we throw off all the shingles, they won't notice." So we spent an hour yanking wooden shingles and tossing them off the roof.

My mom and dad were so mad they didn't let us see each other for a week. Then a few months later they sent me away to a private school in St. John's. It was a cold place full of loud boys wearing blue blazers with silly yellow crests. I was lonely and missed Jess. Finally Christmas came, and when I came back home to Wolf Point for the holiday, Jessica held me tight for a long, long time, and then whispered in my ear, "You're home now."

I didn't go back for another term.

And that was the only time we'd been separated in sixteen years.

But perhaps the strangest thing about the O'Briens was that Jess and her mom were Mormons.

For a long time, the two of them were the only Mormons around. Then her mom got the Hagens and Alberts to join, and every week the three families would get dressed in their Sunday-best and make the boat ride to church. For a reason I can't explain, I always liked watching them leave: the women in their dresses—even Jess cleaned up and looking kind of cute—the men in their suits; all of them standing on the red bow splashing through the dark green ocean toward Basques.

Of course, like everyone in town, I've wondered why the Hagens and Alberts joined—why anyone would join a church just to waste every Sunday boating to Basques and back. Jess took me to church once and there were a couple of cute girls, but the Hagens and Alberts were old and married. I don't get it.

Jess and I have never talked about religion. My family is Catholic, but we only go to church at Christmas and Easter. And for the last few years Jess has been less and less excited about being a Mormon, so I know better than to bring it up. But I wondered about her religion as I stood on the porch that night. Something told me Mr. O'Brien might not come back, and I guessed that Jess would be bitter. I thought she might blame God.

"What's up?" I said into the phone. It was a habit my family always said it.

"Nothing." Jess's typical answer. Her voice was calm. It could have been any conversation on any day. Jess hid her emotions well.

"Um, any news?"

"No. I guess not. Well, we got a call from the Coast Guard or the fish police or someone this morning. They're gonna send a cruiser."

"That's good."

"Yeah."

There was an awkward silence.

"How's your mom?" I asked.

"She's a basket case. Hasn't come out of her room much."

"Huh."

"I took her some breakfast, just toast, but she wouldn't eat it."

"You cry?" I had to know.

"Why would I?"

"Cause your dad's gone."

"He's *not* gone," she snapped into the phone.

"I just meant he's missing, not gone."

I wanted to tell her about the feeling I'd had—that her dad wouldn't be coming back—but something told me not to bring it up. Still, I'd never felt anything like it before. It was eerie.

There was another long silence.

"Well, I better let you go," I said.

"Yeah. Sorry I yelled at you."

"That's okay. It was a dumb thing to say."

"See ya."

21

I dropped the receiver onto the cradle and walked outside. It was a Thursday, and there was no school because it was early August. I thought about going over to Jess's house, but realized I'd probably just feel awkward. So I stepped off the porch and wandered down the road a way.

Megan saw me leave and rushed outside.

"Where ya going?" she called out, leaning over the porch rail. Megan was always hoping I was going somewhere interesting, but I never was.

"Nowhere," I said, turning back to the house and kicking at some pebbles on the road.

"You wanna go down to the pier?"

"No." But then I realized it sounded like something to do. "Maybe."

"Let's go," she said, jumping off the porch and racing past me.

Megan is ten and races a lot of places. She's always moving, doing something. Wolf Point is boring to many people, but not to my little sister. In the summer, she's often gone all day, pulling starfish out of the wading pools or climbing in the rocks around the south shore. I'm six years older than she is, but I often catch myself worrying that Megan thinks I'm boring. Of course, I'd never admit it to her.

Near the corner, Megan stopped abruptly and waited. Her head was tilted up, and I knew she was going to ask something she shouldn't.

"So, what's going on today?"

"Why?" I asked slowly. "What do you mean?"

"Something's going on, but Mom won't tell me."

"You're too young."

"I'm just gonna hear it sooner or later."

I knew she was right. She usually spent part of her day hiding on the cross-beams under the pier, listening to the fishermen talk. I had no doubt that by nightfall she could learn everything there was to know about Jess's dad.

"I don't want Mom blaming me for your scary dreams."

"I won't tell."

I turned down Shoreline and Megan skipped beside.

"It's not a happy thing," I said.

"Someone die?"

"No. Well, I don't know."

"Who?"

"Jess's dad. He went missing yesterday. Didn't come back from fishing."

Megan stopped and looked up at me. It was hard to read her face, but I assumed she didn't know what to feel. She didn't know Mr. O'Brien that well, but she knows Jess. In fact, she worships Jess.

I didn't know what to say, so I started walking again. We passed the last house and then Chern's Store and pretty soon were walking along the main pier listening to the familiar call of the seagulls on the shore. It was late morning, but many of the boats were still in dock. Ed Sapp's boat was first in line, and he was sitting on the deck, cross-legged, feeding a needle and thread through an old, orange net.

"Hi," said Megan. Ed nodded in return.

Next was John Huey, then John Ryan, then Mr. Alexander. Everyone was making repairs today. The weather was nice, but no one was on the water.

Finally we reached the spot where Jess's dad usually moored. The berth was empty, of course. But we both looked over the edge as though we might see something in the water.

"You talk to Jess?" Megan asked.

"Yeah."

"She okay?"

"I don't know. I guess."

I thought about our own dad. He's a botanist with the Canadian Interior Department, so we never have to worry about him disappearing in an ocean storm. Once in a while he takes off for a few days to get some readings in a remote part of the island, but he has a cellular phone and checks in at night. He's pretty tame.

"Got any money?" Megan asked.

"No." I kicked a loose piece of wood into the water.

"I do."

"Where'd you get money?"

"Mom felt bad this morning. Gave me two bucks."

"I didn't get any."

"Nayh, nayh . . . You want something from the store?" she asked.

"Why? What ya gonna buy me?"

Megan shrugged and began skipping back down the pier. I followed, but then looked back to the empty place on the pier and felt a cold chill on my back.

I will remember it forever.

It was the moment that I realized Jessica's childhood was over.

* * * * *

That night, I woke around eleven o'clock. I'd been dreaming about Jess and her father, but it was a disturbing dream. Her dad was walking the beach, but he wasn't the same. I couldn't tell what was different about him, and

24

I didn't want to know. I closed my eyes again and tried to sleep but tossed for an hour or more.

* * * * *

Jess left her house at about midnight. It was a bright night and the sky was full of a white brush of the Milky Way. She walked slowly down to the pier and stood at the same place—where her dad moored. It was cold, and she was wearing a white zip-up sweatshirt with a hood. She stuck her hands deep in the front pocket and waited for something, anything.

About an hour later she woke up. Jessica had sat down and then fallen asleep against one of the old docking posts. The night had turned cold and as black as the velvet in a jewelry box. She had a chill and was even a little scared about being out there all alone in the dark night.

She stood up and was about to turn for home when she saw something from the corner of her eye. Something was moving in the dark, out on the water. There was no light, but for a second the clouds parted and the moonlight broke through, so she could see something against the horizon. It was heading toward her. It could have been a boat, a fishing boat, but it had no lights.

She pulled her hood off and the wind picked up, blowing her brown ponytail around into her face.

Then, from the water, came a voice. It seemed to be traveling slowly by the time it reached the pier, a voice that whispered, unmistakably, "Jess."

The clouds closed around the moon, and the image on the horizon and everything else went dark again. Whatever had been on the water was gone; and so was

Jess. She heard the voice and turned and took off up the pier, back up to Shoreline Drive. She was home in less than a minute, slamming the door behind her so loud it woke every dog for a block.

It would not be the last time she would hear the voice.

5

ARRIVAL

He arrived on the ferry from Basques, just as every-one did who came to Wolf Point. He had been below, but the rocking of the boat began to make him sick, brought a salty taste to his mouth, so he and his new companion excused themselves to a loud salesman and clambered up to the bow to study the passing shore-line in the distance. His stomach settled in the icy wind.

Just before noon, the boat turned and started swim-ming toward a little inlet. From a mile away, he could see a dotting of houses along the rocky shore.

"I think that's it," said the companion, yelling to be heard over the splash of the water and oily roar of the engine.

He nodded and smiled, then looked back at the shore. It was rocky and utterly treeless. He couldn't help think-ing it was an ugly place to come to.

* * * * *

Megan and I were climbing up from the beach when we saw the ferry arrive. She bounded up the last few steps and sprinted along the pier to see if there was any mail or any interesting visitors. There were two of them. One

27

short and one tall—both wearing dark suits and white shirts and ties.

As the taller one strode down the pier in Wolf Point, he stood out like a mail-order catalog model.

Megan fell in step with him. "Hi," she said.

He nodded and stopped.

"Hi, yourself."

His companion caught up, and the two young men continued along the pier. Each carried a bag in one hand and a small leather-bound book in the other. Megan, of course, followed. I went home.

* * * * *

A half-hour later, Megan raced home and burst frantically through our front door.

"Ian!" she yelled.

I didn't answer.

"Iannnn!"

"What?" I had gone down into the basement to watch TV.

Megan yelled a lot. I knew better than to pay much attention; she was always excited about something.

"Get up here," she yelled.

"Yeah, be right there," I yelled back with as much sarcasm as I could muster.

She crashed down the stairs like a falling safe. "I know something you don't know," she said with a cheesy grin.

"Doubt that."

"Oh, yeah? Well those two guys from the ferry are at Jess's house."

"Boy, that *is* news," I replied.

"Ain't you curious?"

"Nope," I lied.

She ran back upstairs, and I peered out the basement

28

window toward the O'Brien's. I couldn't see anything through the bushes, so I climbed the stairs to the kitchen and found Megan sitting at the table. When I appeared, she laughed and jumped up.

"Relax," I said. "They're probably from the coast guard or police or something."

"Oh." Megan thought for a second. "One of them is really cute."

I laughed. "What do you know about cute guys? You're only ten."

She pulled a face at me, then grinned.

I rolled my eyes and walked next door to the O'Brien's house. The two guys were standing on the porch, and as I approached, Jessica opened the door. Then she saw me walking over and waved me away, but I followed them inside anyway. She slugged me in the arm. I gave her a syrupy smile in return.

"Mom," Jessica yelled upstairs. "The missionaries are here."

"Sorry to come at a time like this," the shorter one said. The tall one nodded in agreement.

"Whatever," Jessica said.

"Still no word?" the tall one asked, then looked as though he regretted asking the question.

Jessica shrugged her shoulders. "He's probably stuck on some island or up the coast somewhere."

The missionaries nodded hopefully, but then turned their attention to me.

"Elder Sanchez," said the shorter one.

"Elder Shackelford," said the taller.

They both stuck their hands at me and I shook them. I hadn't shaken many guys' hands in my life. It was pretty cool.

"Ian Blake," I said.

Then we all looked up the stairs, waiting awkwardly for Mrs. O'Brien to appear.

"She'll probably be down in a minute," said Jessica. "I'll get you some lemonade or something."

"Sure, thanks."

"None for you, nosy boy," she said to me, and disappeared into the kitchen. She seemed happy to get away.

Elder Shackelford leaned close to his companion after the kitchen door swung shut. "Someone's in denial," he whispered, but I overheard him.

Elder Sanchez nodded back.

They looked at family pictures on the wall until Mrs. O'Brien appeared at the head of the stairs. She smiled thinly at the two young men. She was wearing a big, woolen cardigan and her hair was done up in curls, like a pile of loose, brown chair springs.

"Afternoon, boys."

"Afternoon," they replied in unison.

"Picked a nice day to arrive in town," she said climbing slowly down the staircase.

"Yep," said Sanchez. "Perfect weather. The water was a little choppy, but not bad."

They all shook hands in front of the piano. Then she saw me and shook my hand too. Her hand was cold.

"It was my first boat ride," Elder Shackelford said. "Pretty fun."

"Just like riding in a car to us, son," Sister O'Brien said. "Have a seat."

They sat on the O'Brien's old tan sofa, and I sat on the piano bench. Mrs. O'Brien took the high-backed chair near the window and looked outside. No one spoke for a while. They waited for Mrs. O'Brien to turn away from the window.

"Now I've met Elder Sanchez, but you're new around here," she finally said, looking at the taller one.

"I'm Elder Shackelford. I've only been in the mission a few months."

"Are you liking it?"

"Like no place else on earth," he said.

"Good answer. And where are you from?"

"Montreal."

"Beautiful city," she said. "We were thinking of taking a trip to Montreal and Toronto in the fall. My husband loved hockey. So does Jessica. They wanted to watch a few games, and I thought I could shop." She laughed lightly and put on a brave face, but it looked forced. We all smiled at her.

"Great shops in Montreal," Elder Shackelford said after another awkward silence.

"So," she said, "are you boys in town for a while? It's been a long stretch since we've had missionaries here full-time."

"President Gates assigned us here for a few weeks," said Sanchez. "He said you'd find enough people to keep us busy teaching."

"I should think so. It'll help take my mind off . . . well, it'll keep me busy."

She looked around the room, "Where's Jessica?" she asked me.

"Making them lemonade," I answered.

"She hasn't taken this well," said Mrs. O'Brien to the missionaries.

Sanchez leaned forward. "She obviously has great faith

that her father is . . . well, alive. But President Gates told us they've stopped the search."

"He's gone," she said, her voice filled with a deep sadness. "Everyone here . . . every family knows the risks of this life. Jessica just refuses to accept it."

"We like to tell people that families are forever," Shackelford said, smiling. "We could talk to her about the plan of salvation and eternal life. You were all sealed in the temple?"

"My husband wasn't a member," said Mrs. O'Brien, dropping her gaze.

"Oh. I'm sorry."

Jessica pushed through the door and handed each of the elders a glass. She grabbed her coat and pulled me toward the front door.

"I've got plans, and it doesn't involve sitting around and finding victims for the missionaries," she whispered to me, but I think everyone heard.

"Be back later," she said to her mom.

"Where are you two going?" Mrs. O'Brien asked.

"Out on Ian's boat."

"Be careful, and don't leave the harbor."

And we were gone.

As we walked down toward the ocean I could see Jessica's mom looking out the window. She was watching the horizon. It was clear.

* * * * *

"So who were they?" I asked when we got to the beach.

"Who?"

"You know who. The guys at your house. Megan thought they were cute."

Jessica guffawed. "They're just missionaries. They're

annoying. They're always looking to baptize someone or comfort some grieving family."

She grabbed a side of my boat. "Let's get this into the water."

"I thought missionaries went to Africa."

She shrugged. It was obvious she didn't want to talk, so I grabbed hold and we dragged the small boat across the gravelly shore and jumped in. I pulled the starter a few times before the little outboard jumped to life. I took the stern and Jess the bow.

"What are missionaries doing here?" I asked while we were still chugging through the harbor.

"They want to convert the world, . . . but they'd start with you."

I laughed.

"I'm serious. They want all of you to become Mormons."

"I wouldn't join."

Jess shook her head. "They all say that. That's what Dutch Hagen said, and he joined."

"So?"

We reached the head of the harbor, and I turned north into a stiff ocean wind, the same wind we'd faced all week as we searched every inch of coastline for ten miles.

"North again?" I asked. "He could have gone south, you know."

"He went north. I saw him."

"Yeah, but maybe he hit bad weather going north and doubled back. Wouldn't hurt to try south."

"There was no weather to hit. It was clear. Just go north."

This time we kept away from land in an attempt to get as far north as possible and search new territory. She kept her binoculars on the rocky shore and only broke her watch every now and then to wipe the lenses clear of salt-water spray. After an hour, I was bored and hungry.

"You bring anything to eat?" I asked.

She shot me a nasty look, but calmed quickly. I was, after all, helping out. She shook her head.

"Any gum?"

"Nope."

"I don't think much of your cruise line."

"You can always swim back," she offered.

"Or you could."

She went back to watching the shore. I thought of something to ask, which is what I do best at times like that.

"So," I said, grasping for the strangest thing my mind could imagine, "you ever eat something that was still alive?"

Jess set down her binoculars. "I'd have to think about that. Do bugs count?"

"Yeah, but not accidental eatings, like when you swallow a fly on your bike."

"How about plants. They're still alive."

"No. I mean an animal or a bug—something from the insect or animal kingdoms—but something that you meant to eat alive."

Jess shrugged. "I guess not. How about you?"

"Nope. I don't think so. Megan says she once ate a little fish out of a tidal pool."

"Gross."

"She said she was hungry. She was way down by the Telephone Rock."

Jessica shuddered. "It'd swim around in your stomach," she said, crinkling her nose.

"Not for long," I added.

"Yuck."

My mind raced for another question.

"Um," I said, a little bit nervous. "I got a question . . . I guess."

I was silent for a second.

"Yeah?" she asked.

"Well. It was something Megan said." I paused again. "Um . . . well, she said the guys, the missionaries, were cute."

"What's your question?"

"Well, did you think they were cute?"

"What?" she blushed.

"You heard me. Anyway, you never tell me if you think guys are cute."

"I don't know any guys."

"Thanks."

"Anyway, they're not guys, they're missionaries."

"So they're *not* guys."

"No."

"So what makes a guy cute?" I was warming to this subject matter.

"I don't know. I don't want to talk about this."

"Tough. It's my boat."

"You just said it was my cruise line."

"I'm the captain. Answer the question."

She lifted the binoculars to her face and took another scan of the shoreline. It was obvious she wasn't about to give this information out without a fight.

"You like blue eyes?" I asked finally.

She shrugged. "They're okay."

"Well, do you have a preference in eye color?"

"No. Blue's fine. Brown. Paisley. I don't care."

"Tall, short?" I asked.

"Medium." She smiled slyly.

"So you're not particular. Okay, how about . . . um. What else is there?"

"Sense of humor. He'd have to have a good sense of humor," she volunteered.

"Of course." I couldn't help notice my pulse racing in my throat. I was enjoying this dialogue, and I didn't know why. "Hair color preference? Wealthy guy? Anything else you are looking for? Or just a medium-sized guy with a sense of humor."

"Guess I'm not too picky. I just hate . . ."

"What?"

"Nothing."

"You can't do that. Tell me."

"Oh, I was just gonna say I hate pretty guys."

I laughed so hard that for a while I lost control of the outboard.

* * * * *

Some time after noon we reached unfamiliar ground and Jess had me steer in close to shore. I picked my way around the tall, black rocks that rose out of the water like thick fingers, while Jessica watched for signs of a boat washed up on the break. We both knew what was coming a few miles ahead, but neither of us spoke of it.

The outboard made a monotonous hum, and there was a steady wash of water against the bow, but otherwise it was quiet. Another hour passed before the water slowly started changing color from almost black to a strange swirling green. We looked ahead to see the land start edging out slightly into the sea. We were coming to a dark, rocky point that looked menacingly like the end of the earth.

36

It *was* the end of the earth, according to most residents of Wolf Point.

The cove had been named after the *Ballycater* that sunk there in 1856. And Ballycater Cove had a reputation among the locals, who were a superstitious group to begin with. That reputation may have started with that fateful sinking, but it was enhanced by the almost constant fog that hung over the shoreline, hiding the cluster of jagged rocks that were hidden under the water. In the 150 years since the *Ballycater* sank, the treacherous cove had sent more than its share of boats to a watery grave.

Megan had overheard John Huey talking on the pier once and had passed the information along to me. John had said that as a young boy he'd fished in Ballycater and caught a week's catch in a few hours. But, he said, the fog just about caught him. And as he sped away from the evil-looking place, he thought he heard voices behind him.

Megan said the others took it as fact. She said that Mr. Alexander had proclaimed that everyone knew Ballycater was haunted, and John Huey was lucky to have survived with his head still on his neck.

I turned the little boat further into the ocean, and slowly we rounded the bend. The ocean was swirling in patterns of that same deep green. I killed the engine and the boat settled into the rock of the swells.

Then we looked into the mouth of Ballycater Cove.

The inlet was about a mile wide and twice as deep. Jutting up in the cove was a chessboard of jagged rocks, hinting of the danger that lay below. The far shore was lost to a heavy fog that rolled off the land in waves.

"Well?" I asked, but Jessica didn't answer. She was looking deep into the cove.

"It's getting late," I said.

I looked up at the sun. We had just enough time to get home before dark—maybe.

"There are a lot of rocks in there. Your dad would never go in with his trawler," I told her. But even then I couldn't be sure. This stretch of the coast had been almost fished out, and men like Mr. O'Brien had been known to do crazy things if it meant bringing in a decent harvest—even venturing into a haunted cove.

Jessica pointed into Ballycater. "You see that patch of land, the green patch?"

"No."

"There."

Then I saw it. Showing through a break in the fog was a small stretch of shore at the farthest point inland.

"Yeah."

"Let's just go there and then head back."

"We'll get stuck in the fog. You ever get lost in fog?" I asked.

"You scared or something?"

"No, I just like my boat."

"It'll be fine. Just go slow."

I breathed deep and fired up the outboard. I advanced the throttle slightly, and the boat inched into the cove.

"Watch the water for rocks," I said.

Jessica leaned over the bow and stared into the green water.

＊　＊　＊　＊　＊

We both felt the chill coming. We were only half way in when it washed over the boat, followed by a fog that quickly grew as thick as wool.

"I can't see the water," Jessica finally said and looked back at me, but I was surrounded by a veil of mist. I killed the engine and the boat rocked in the hidden water.

"Maybe it'll clear in a minute," I said.

But the fog didn't break. It rolled in heavy, weighing down the boat—confining, frightening.

"You have a compass?" Jessica finally asked.

"No." I replied, and my voice echoed.

I said "no" again, this time louder just to hear the word echo. My voice came back quicker.

"We're getting near land," I said.

"Or a rock," whispered Jessica.

We sat still for a minute, uncertain. Steadily the waves began picking up intensity and direction. Salt-water spray hit our faces and we heard the crash of water against something solid. Suddenly the fog broke long enough for us to see a rock towering above us, rising high out of the water.

"Do something. Start the engine," Jessica yelled, hanging on to the side of the rocking boat.

I pulled the outboard motor and it sputtered to life. "Grab an oar," I said.

Jessica pulled the wood oar out of the boat bottom and slipped it into the water. I eased the throttle and we jumped a swell.

Bump. We came down hard on a submerged part of the rock, but the metal bottom held and Jessica pushed us off with the oar. I gave the outboard more power and we jumped another wave, then another. Soon the water calmed and we were clear of the rock, but still in the thick fog.

"I don't know where to go," I admitted.

"Got another one," said Jessica, her oar touching the top of another rock. "Slow down."

I eased back the throttle, and the boat slowed. Jessica pushed off, and we continued, picking our way slowly across the cove. It was quiet except for the hum of the motor and the splash of water against the boat. The silence seemed to grow in circles around us, getting heavier and more ominous.

Suddenly, Jess froze. Her eyes opened wide and she stared at me. She looked petrified.

"What?" I asked.

She didn't speak. She sat rigidly in the boat, as though listening for something.

"What is it?" I asked again.

Her mouth dropped open, and I finally recognized her fear. I jammed the throttle full-open and the boat jumped forward. The oar almost slipped out of Jess's hand, and she instinctively pulled it in. I knew it was insane, but I made a panicked rush for daylight.

We rumbled over a rock, and I thought about slowing, but then ahead we saw it—a small break in the fog. A few seconds later we pushed through into daylight and found ourselves out almost to open sea—out of the cove. Without slowing I turned south.

I was embarrassed by my panic. Neither of us spoke for nearly an hour.

"Humph," I said at last, just a noise to break the silence between us.

Jessica looked up. "Humph," she echoed, and ran her hand through her damp hair.

"So, uh, what happened back there?" I asked.

"I don't know."

"You looked like you'd seen a ghost."

"No," she said, studying my face. "You hear anything in the cove?"

"Like what?"

"I don't know. Anything?"

"Not a thing. What'd you hear," I asked.

"Nothing. Probably a bird or something."

"What did it sound like?"

"You'd laugh."

"Not today, I wouldn't."

"It sounded . . . I don't know, it sounded like somebody was calling my name."

I put my hand up to my chin and rubbed. "That's spooky."

"Yeah. And you know what? It kind of sounded like my dad. I think my dad was calling me."

I didn't know how to respond.

"He's in there," Jess said. "He's in Ballycater."

6

CHERN'S PLACE

The missionaries stayed in the only room for rent in Wolf Point, located above Chern's store. Of course, Chern's place was actually much more than a hotel or general store—it was the post office, the ferry office, and the meeting place for the locals, especially when new faces landed.

Elder Shackelford and Elder Sanchez had most likely expected to spend their first night in a member's home, eating fresh-caught seafood and talking about prospective "golden contacts." Instead, Miles Chern grabbed them by their arms when they returned to the store and said they'd be eating in his little cafe that night, no questions asked. He had a lot of people coming by, and he wasn't about to disappoint them.

At seven, the missionaries climbed down the stairs and wound their way through the maze of whitewashed stone hallways—following the sound of loud talk and laughter. There was no door on the cafe, and they walked inside to see at least two dozen men—all wearing plaid—seated at four or five tables crammed into a room barely larger than a Volkswagen bus. The room was heavy with smoke, and in front of each man was a large glass of beer. I was hidden in the back, sitting beside my dad. I wasn't about to miss their interrogation, either.

The talking and laughter stopped abruptly as the missionaries entered, wearing their dark suits.

"No need to dress for dinner, boys," said Chern, and the group laughed heartily.

"This is our usual attire," Shackelford answered.

They moved into the room and a couple of the younger locals jumped up to give them chairs. The missionaries sat down uncertainly, squeezing their shoulders into place at one of the tables.

"We have stew," said Chern, nodding at them.

"Thanks, yes," replied Sanchez. "And water."

Chern disappeared into the kitchen and the missionaries sat awkwardly, looking down at the empty coffee cups in front of them.

"So you boys from the mainland?" asked Morgan Boudreau, an older local with amazingly deep wrinkles on his face—like mountain ranges on a globe.

"I'm from Texas . . . from Austin. And Elder Shackelford is from Montreal," said Sanchez.

"Texas!"

"Yes."

"Remember the Alamo," said Miles Einersten, a huge young guy at the end of their table. Everyone laughed again, and the missionaries smiled, though it was obvious they didn't find it very funny.

"And they say you're Mormons," said the older guy as he lit a pipe.

The two young men looked at each other. Obviously word traveled fast in our little town.

"Yes, we're here to share the gospel of Jesus Christ," Sanchez said. Shackelford nodded helpfully.

43

"I know the Bible well enough, I think," said Morgan, shaking out a match with one knarled hand and taking a long puff on his pipe. There were grunts of agreement from around the room.

"No doubt, but our church believes in modern-day revelation," Sanchez explained. "And a modern-day prophet."

The room was quiet. Everyone was soaking in what Sanchez had said and feeling awkward.

"Probably sounds kind of strange," Shackelford finally added.

"It does," said old Morgan. "Sounds a bit like a cult."

Elder Shackelford smiled. "That's what I used to think. But it's true . . . it's the true church. I wouldn't have given up two years of my life to serve if I didn't believe that with all my heart."

"Two years?" asked Miles, the big man at the end of the table. He wore thick suspenders and had a shaggy, brown beard. Shackelford nodded at him, but Miles sneered back.

Elder Sanchez said, "Elder Shackelford passed up a chance to play professional hockey for the Montreal . . . what are they called?"

"Canadiens," said his companion quietly.

"Right, the Canadiens. He gave that up to serve."

The room was silent for only a moment. Then a young man in the back said, "I know him. I saw him in a junior game in Halifax a couple of years back. Ernie Shackelford, right?"

"Eddy."

The young man stood up and raised his beer mug. "Fastest skater I've ever seen." He turned to the crowd.

"Scored a hat trick before the end of the first period. It was something to see."

Elder Shackelford looked at his hands and twirled his fork.

"You gave up a shot with the Habs?" asked Miles.

The big elder smiled. "Hockey was my life for a long time. But I have a chance to do something here that is more important."

"This here is Canada. There's nothing more important than hockey," Miles said, and the room erupted in laughter. He looked around, grinning with satisfaction, and someone called out, "Good one, Miles."

"Oh, I know of one thing," Shackelford said, and the room fell silent.

But big Miles was not finished. He hooked his thumbs behind his suspenders and leaned back in his chair. It creaked under the weight of his impressive frame. "You know what I think?" he asked. "I think this guy is full of it. He sure ain't no hockey player."

Shackelford smiled. "I'm probably not, by now."

"Miles played junior hockey in St. John's," said the young man in the back.

"Miles sat in penalty boxes all over eastern Canada," said Morgan, and the room erupted in laughter again, and Miles flushed with anger.

"So," Elder Shackelford said, changing the subject when the laughter died down, "how did Wolf Point gets its name?"

"My great-grandfather named this outpost," said Morgan, taking a puff of his pipe, "after a wolf he saw while hunting just inland. The story goes, he was—"

"That's not true and you know it, Morgan," said Chern, coming out from behind the bar with two bowls of stew.

"My ancestors were here in the 1800s, boys. They named the town New Wolf Point, because they'd come from a Wolf Point back in England."

"Ah, nonsense," said Morgan, puffing his pipe furiously.

"You've both got seaweed in your heads," said my dad. He leaned across and thumped on the missionaries' table with his finger end. "This village was founded by Blakes, my people, back in 1743. They named it after a rock outcropping that looked like a wolf. You probably noticed it on the way in, just to the south of the bay."

Elder Shackleford saw me seated behind my dad and winked.

"That's rubbish, Blake," said Morgan, loudly. "We settled this outpost in the 1600s, just ten years after Champlain arrived in Canada. We dropped the first fishing net into the water off this coast."

"Well, you may have put the first fishing net in the water, but the Blakes caught the first fish . . . and we didn't get here until 1743," said my dad, and everyone laughed.

Elder Shackelford found himself laughing with the locals, but stopped when he noticed the large furry face of Miles Einersten staring back at him with cold, clear eyes. The big elder looked down. He seemed more annoyed than afraid.

The evening seemed to go slowly for the sober elders, and sometime after nine they excused themselves and returned to their room overlooking the bay.

* * * * *

The next morning I was on the beach early. I'd pulled my boat out of the water, flipped it over, and was inspecting the metal hull closely—running my fingers over every

46

inch in a search for new bumps and gashes from the rocks in Ballycater Cove. By the time my sister wandered down the shoreline I'd had found at least three large dents in the metal and was in a foul mood.

"What's up?" Megan asked.

I glared at her in response, then went back to feeling the boat.

"Wow! Where'd you get this big dent?" She put her hand on the aluminum hull.

"Nowhere."

"Maybe a fish bumped into you." She tried to smile at me, but I didn't flinch, just kept running my hand along the boat.

Finally I stood up and turned the boat over.

"Why don't you go do something else?" I asked and then climbed inside.

"Nothing else to do. Anyway, I know you've been up to something and I want to know what. I'm not leaving until you tell me."

"Fine."

"I mean it. I'm going to follow you all day."

"Fine."

She sat down on the beach and watched me inspect the bottom of the boat—crawling around on my hands and knees.

"Lose your gum?" she asked and laughed.

I didn't reply, but I couldn't help grinning slightly. I shook it off, but she had noticed the break in my armor and wasn't about to give up.

"Maybe you're practicing getting seasick."

"Go away."

"I've got it. You're praying that your little dingy will be turned into a real boat."

"That's it—" I jumped out of the boat and raced for her. "You're going in the ocean."

She was up before I reached her and began sprinting down the beach. In spite of her head start, I caught her easily and reached an arm around her tiny waist. Megan is as light as a bag of cotton, and I raced to the water with her under one arm. She made a half-terrified, half-laughing wailing sound—like the old World War II air siren at Chern's store—as she wiggled and kicked to get free.

Just before the water I stopped and pretended to get ready to throw her in. She stopped squirming and demanded, "You'd better not."

I was torn and Megan knew it. For her, this made it really fun. If I put her down, rules of sisterhood decreed that she could taunt me all day. If I decided to throw her in, I knew full well that she'd run home and tell Mom, and I'd be in big trouble.

For a ten-year-old sister, there was no better position to be in. She would win either way.

"Don't you dare throw her in," came a voice from behind.

We both turned our heads to see Jessica walking up the beach barefoot, carrying a pair of brown sandals in one hand.

I thought for a second, made another mock attempt to throw Megan in to the surf, but eventually set her down on the sand. She ran over to Jessica and they sat on the edge of my boat. Jessica crossed her legs and Megan, watching her, did the same.

"What's up?" I asked.

"Nothing. Been wading," said Jessica, holding up her sandals. "You guys wanna walk up the beach?"

"Ian can't put his feet in the water," said Megan. "Dad said the pollution would kill all the fish around Newfoundland."

Jessica laughed half-heartedly.

"Hardy, har, har," from me, but I smiled and sat on the wet sand to pull off my hiking boots and socks. I stretched out a pair of long, thick, pale feet for inspection.

"I don't know that I've ever seen anything that white," said Jessica, and Megan laughed.

I stared down at my feet and nodded. "They kind of look like something you'd find when you turn over a rock." And all three of us laughed. It was probably the first time I'd heard Jessica laugh in weeks.

An hour later we were wading along the shore. Megan ran on ahead to chase seagulls when Jessica broke the news.

"We're broke," she confided to me.

I looked down at the water, not sure what to say.

"Mom said she was supposed to get some insurance money, but she can only get that if Dad's dead. And he's not."

The police had officially listed her father as drowned, but I didn't want to remind her of that or ask why the insurance company didn't believe them.

"You need something?" I finally asked. "You need food or something?"

"We're not starving. We're just broke."

"Sorry, I didn't mean to—"

"No, I'm sorry. I just wish Dad were here," she said, turning her face away.

We looked out into the bay, as if we expected his trawler to sail around the channel buoy at any moment.

After awhile we caught up with Megan next to the

brown and gray rock wall that bordered the tail end of Shoreline Drive. We spotted the missionaries in their dark suits and white shirts from a half mile away, knocking on every door along Shoreline and getting turned politely away by every housewife. Finally, the two young men stopped to watch a pick-up game of street hockey a few local kids were playing.

"He's a hockey player," I said.

Megan waved frantically and called out to Elder Shackelford, but her voice was lost to the overwhelming screech of the seagulls.

"I know," said Megan. She grinned and I realized she'd been eavesdropping under the pier again. "Someone said he could've been a star, but Miles Einersten says he's a fake," she added and started waving again.

"Miles is a bully and a know-it-all," said Jessica.

"Come on," said Megan, and she raced over the soft sand and up the stone staircase in the quay. Jessica and I followed reluctantly. We met up with the missionaries in front of the Scotts' place, a slanting white frame house that looked ready to blow over with a good enough gust. Sanchez shook hands with all of us, but Shackelford was mesmerized by the hockey game.

"Morning," said Elder Sanchez.

"Hi," said Megan, smiling brightly at the tall, handsome figure of Shackelford.

"Nice day," he said, turning briefly to us. "Keep your stick on the ground," he called to one of the little players.

Megan giggled and picked up a pair of old hockey sticks that were lying in the grass on the side of the road.

"You wanna play?" she asked Elder Shackelford.

He looked over at Sanchez for some sort of guidance, but then shook his head. "Nah, I better not."

Sanchez nodded and added, "Probably not." But Shackelford had already taken a stick from Megan and was twirling it in his hands, caressing the rough wood.

"Well . . . maybe." He walked into the middle of the game. "Mind if I just take a shot or two?" he asked the kids. He looked to be in a trance. The kids made way to let the big guy in the dark suit play.

"Err, okay," one said, flipping him the tennis ball. Eddy caught the ball on the stick blade and batted it in the air a few times. Without letting it hit the ground he sent a bullet of a shot into the top corner of the kids' net. The boy playing goal swallowed hard and inched to one side.

"I'm on his team," said Megan, and every one of the little kids echoed with, "I'm on his team too."

"No, no," said Eddy, looking for someone to hand the stick to. "I really can't. We've got work to do." But the kids begged.

"Just five minutes of play," he reasoned with his companion. "I haven't played in months."

He scooped the ball out of the net and knocked it ahead. A mass of little players swarmed around the ball, but Eddy swooped in and stole it away, dancing around the boys—scoring one quick goal and then another. Then he got Megan involved, sending her a bullet pass that knocked the stick out of her hand but sent the ball directly into the net.

"You see that?" she asked me. I rolled my eyes at her, but it was impressive. I'd never seen anyone do such incredible things with a hockey stick.

Five and then ten minutes passed. A small crowd had gathered. A few of the housewives had come out to watch this strange young man in a suit score goals on their kids.

51

And a couple of the fishermen who weren't out on the water had wandered home for lunch and were watching.

One of them was Miles Einersten.

Eddy nodded awkwardly, but Miles didn't acknowledge the gesture—just stared right through Eddy, wearing a deep scowl on his young bearded face.

"I guess we'd better get back to work," Eddy said, wiping his forehead with the back of a suit arm.

"Nonsense," said old Morgan, taking a seat on Mrs. Scott's stone fence and taking his pipe out of its pouch. "Have a go against Roger and Miles, here." He pointed toward Miles and another young burly fisherman, Roger DePeel, who was leaning against a lamppost with his sleeves rolled up over club-like forearms.

Eddy straightened. "I better not," he said, looking at Sanchez for advice.

"I could teach him a thing or two," said Roger, grabbing a stick out of a young boy's hands.

The big elder shrugged and flipped him the tennis ball. Roger took the ball on his stick blade and rumbled like a rhinoceros in suspenders toward Eddy and the waiting goal. Without looking Eddy flicked his stick out, caught the ball and flipped it through Roger's legs. He picked the ball up behind the stunned man and shot it thirty feet into the empty goal.

"Hey, I wasn't ready," Roger protested.

"Sorry," said Eddy, grinning.

Roger ran back heavily to the net and fished out the ball. He walked slowly up the road and then sprinted when he reached Eddy, but the result was the same. Eddy ended up with the tennis ball as Roger spun in circles trying to catch him.

"Sit down, Rogg," said Miles. He threw his coat to the

side of the road and snatched the hockey stick out of Roger's hands. He held the stick out and looked down the shaft, like a pool player looks down his stick. Then he banged the stick against the ground a few times.

Eddy fired a pass to him and Miles had to move fast to take it on his stick blade. He had pretty quick reflexes for a big guy.

Miles walked up the road toward Eddy's goal, stick-handling the ball crisply back and forth. He was a hockey player, that was clear. When he reached the missionary he threw his back into him and maneuvered around him, then broke for the net. Eddy reacted quickly and caught Miles in two steps. Their sticks collided and the ball floated in the air for a second as Eddy dodged toward his goal and took up position. Miles waited for the ball to stop bouncing and then sent a heavy slapshot toward Eddy's net. As soon as the shot was released Eddy ducked. The ball shot just over his head, well above the goal.

"Yikes," said Sanchez.

"No harm done," said Eddy, running back to retrieve the ball. "I needed a haircut."

Miles said nothing, just walked back toward his net to get ready for Eddy's offense. Eddy brought the ball up the street and spun in front of the goal, slipping it easily into the top of the net with a smooth backhand shot. Megan cheered wildly.

Miles pulled the ball out of the net, flipped it ahead and began accelerating up the road. Eddy backed up until he was almost in the goal crease and waited. When Miles reached the halfway point he pulled the ball to a stop and wound up for another slapshot. This one stayed low to the ground. It seemed Eddy had a fix on it. He even started to move his stick to deflect it aside, but then stopped. The ball snapped into the back of the netting.

"Yes!" said Miles.

Eddy banged his stick on the ground in what looked to me like mock frustration, then smiled. "That's some shot you've got."

Miles couldn't help grinning. "Thanks," he mumbled.

Eddy walked up to the big fisherman and stuck his hand out. "Always nice to meet a fellow hockey player," he said.

Miles hesitated and then grudgingly took Elder Shackelford's hand and they shook. Then Miles tossed his stick to one of the kids and walked on toward his house.

Elder Shackelford relinquished his stick and joined us on the sidelines.

"You're really good," said Megan.

The elder smiled at her and then changed the subject. "Actually, we were hoping to meet up with you again," he said to Jessica. "We thought that maybe we could have a talk."

"I'm pretty busy."

"We wouldn't take much of your time," added Sanchez. "We could even do it now, maybe walk on the beach with you. Maybe your friends could wait. We'll just take a minute."

Jessica looked around. She met my gaze and I shrugged.

"Just say whatever it is in front of them," she said.

Sanchez and his companion looked at each other. Finally, Sanchez said, "Um, er, we were just wondering if . . . um . . . you think your friends would like to listen to the discussions?"

She shook her head. "They're not interested."

Megan and I had no idea what they were talking about. Megan just grinned at Elder Shackelford like a fool. I tried to maintain a neutral expression.

"I don't suppose it would hurt to ask," said Sanchez, looking at us.

"Leave them alone, okay. They're my only friends."

"Sorry. I was . . ." Sanchez turned to Shackelford and turned his palms into the air as a sign for help.

"What kind of bird is that?" Elder Shackelford asked, pointing down to the beach to a waddling, white bird the size of a goose.

"A seagull," Megan answered helpfully.

"What? Don't you have seagulls in Montreal?" Elder Sanchez asked his companion.

"Yeah. Just not that big. It's huge."

"They get fat eating fish guts off the pier," said Megan.

Elder Shackelford grunted. "That's a big bird. The sumo wrestler of seagulls."

"He could carry off small dogs," agreed Sanchez.

Megan laughed.

"So is that all you guys wanted, to get my friends?" Jessica asked.

Sanchez nodded at his companion to speak.

"No," said Shackelford. "We wanted to talk to you about your father. We wanted to know that if you have any questions about . . . well, about the afterlife. About where your father is now and how you can be close to him."

"Nope." Jessica spun around and walked down the steps to the beach.

"The other day we kind of got the feeling that you think he's still alive," said Sanchez to her back.

"He is."

55

"It's good to have hope," Elder Shackelford said, as we all hurried to catch up with her. "We don't want to take your hope away, we just wanted to let you know that we're here to talk—any time."

"Great."

"And we want you to know that your Heavenly Father loves you and your mother," said Shackelford, fumbling out the words. I felt for him. It's tough to offer comfort to anyone, especially to Jessica.

Jessica stopped and curled her toes into the sand. I could see she was fuming.

"Don't ever say that," she muttered, closing her eyes and drawing her lips into a tight line.

"What?" asked Elder Shackelford.

Turning to face him, she said, "I said don't ever lie to me. You want me to believe my dad is dead, and then you tell me that God loves me. If He loved me, my dad would be here. Do you know how that makes me feel, you saying that?"

"No," said the elder. "I don't."

"We're sorry," said Sanchez. "We didn't mean to cause more harm. We'll just shut up now."

"Thank you."

That's all that was said for a while. We stood in silence on the beach as the morning wore on, all watching Jessica look out to sea.

I wasn't sure what she was thinking at that moment, but I imagined she was trying not to feel alone and small compared with the huge granite-colored ocean that spread like darkness for miles and miles before her. For years, the sea had given her family life. Now, it had taken her father from her.

But I knew she wasn't going to give him up without a

fight. She was hanging by the smallest of threads to hope, but she wouldn't let the pain win. She had always been strong. Stronger than me, stronger than anyone I'd ever known.

None of us said anything. The only sound was the sad whisper of the wind blowing off the ocean.

7

A LIGHT

Megan was the first to break the silence. She whispered in my ear, and I shrugged. "Megan wants to show you guys something," I said. Shackelford and Sanchez nodded happily.

"It's up the shore," Megan said, rubbing her hands and adding as much mystery as her little voice could muster.

"Okay," said Elder Shackelford.

"You'll have to climb some," she added.

"We'll manage."

"You coming?" I asked Jessica.

She didn't answer, but she did follow as we climbed up the quay and then followed the rock wall along the beach. Shackelford and Sanchez walked in front with Megan in the middle. I dropped behind to be with Jessica. As we walked Megan talked, pointing out algae and birds along the shoreline. Until that moment I had never realized how much a part of this place she is.

"You wanna guess what it is?" Megan said over her shoulder. She ran ahead and jumped on a boulder.

Elder Shackelford just smiled, and Sanchez did a puzzled thing with his hands.

It was a game of suspense, and Megan asked the

question several more times on the way. Our five figures moved quickly through the humid air of the warm afternoon. We left the beach behind and began walking over a rough trail on the rocky north bend. The elders looked hot and uncomfortable in their suits and ties.

"No hints?" asked Shackelford, and Megan answered him with a serious expression and a shake of her head.

"Fine," he said. "Fine."

Megan disappeared behind a rock outcropping and the rest of us followed, all except Sanchez who was staring down at his shoes, which were covered with wet sand. He brushed off what he could and jogged after. He caught up with us, but Megan was gone.

We looked around for a second. Finally, Jessica noticed Megan some fifty yards away—lying on her stomach beside a large tidal pool.

"Hey!" yelled Elder Sanchez. She didn't move.

Sanchez got ready to yell again, but his companion said, "Shhhh!"

"What? She's just hiding from us."

Elder Shackelford shook his head and walked quietly over to my sister, who never took her eyes off the pool.

"It's here, isn't it?" Elder Shackelford asked her.

"How do you like 'em," said Megan. She looked around eagerly. "No one else knows about this place."

We squinted at the water, looking to find the thing Megan had brought us to see. The bottom of the tidal pool seemed barren, a dirty brown expanse covered with specks of red and gray. On the far side were a few clumps of wild grass and more rock.

"What is it?" Elder Shackelford asked.

"You don't see?" asked Megan. She began to snicker,

then got up, pulled off her shoes and stepped into the pool.

"Follow me," she said, a few steps in.

Jessica and I obeyed, pulling off our shoes and socks and stepping gingerly into the lukewarm water. The elders hesitated for a time, looking at each other before removing their shoes and socks and rolling up their trouser legs.

The five of us stopped when we reached the middle of the pool and looked at Megan for some sort of direction. A cool breeze was blowing now, but our feet felt warm in the tidal water. I could still hear the call of the seagulls and, faraway, the sounding of the bell on the channel buoy.

"So?" I asked, impatiently.

Megan smiled. "Look in the water."

We did—focusing through the murky water on the mass of tiny, gray shapes. Each of us looked around and around and then back to the shore. That's when I noticed the gray specks had parted where we had walked. Everyone noticed it at the same time. We all froze in place.

"Crabs!" said Sanchez. He couldn't move.

"Yeah," said Megan, smiling happily, standing amid hundreds of small, crawling shellfish. "Isn't it great!"

Sanchez edged back toward his shoes, placing each foot carefully, until he came to a long rock high enough to stand on. Then he jumped out of the water and threw himself onto the overhang. Jessica followed and pulled herself out of the water. Shackelford and I and Megan remained standing in the middle of the pool.

"This has to be the most disgusting thing I've ever seen," Sanchez said, regaining his composure, but staring intently at the mass of crawling crabs moving around in the bottom of the pool.

I noticed Sanchez's toes twitching. "How could there be so many?" he asked.

Megan picked up a large red crab by its shell. "They can't bite you," she added with amusement. "You know, when you pick 'em up this way."

"This is . . . weird," Elder Shackelford said.

Below us the water swarmed with life, and for some odd reason it was a thing of immense interest. Megan had obviously already figured that out, along with the fact that the multitude of crabs, sunning themselves in the warmth of the pool, were completely harmless.

Megan was collecting a couple of the larger crabs, scooping up those near her, when she pushed her brown hair back from her eyes and looked up at Elder Shackelford.

"What'd you think?" she asked.

"Interesting." he smiled and said, "Thanks for sharing this with us."

Megan smiled. "This place is magical," she said. "I just wanted you to see it, that's all."

"It *is* a magical place," he said. He paused for a moment, then said, "The founder of our church, Joseph Smith, went to a grove of trees to pray when he was about your age, maybe a little older. He was visited by Heavenly Father and the Savior. I bet that was *his* magical place. Maybe not so different from here."

Jessica rolled her eyes. "Missionaries are so obvious."

Elder Shackelford laughed. "I guess that's true. We have a tendency to relate *everything* to the gospel. You get that way when you live and breathe this stuff."

"I bet nobody believed him, huh?" asked Megan.

"Who, Joseph Smith?"

Megan nodded.

"Well, the people who didn't know him didn't believe him," Elder Shackelford said.

"I know how that feels," she said.

I swallowed with guilt. Megan had told me about this place and I'd laughed.

"They really don't mind if you pick then up?" I asked, pushing my hand into the water and grabbing a small Red tightly. "Just don't pick them up by their claws, huh?"

"Sage advice," said Elder Sanchez as he picked his way off the ledge and slowly closer toward the water and the moving mass of shellfish. Megan looked at the timid elder and laughed. She jumped into the air and splashed down hard, then began running around the pool, herding the crabs like a sheep dog.

Everyone laughed, even Jessica.

And for a time, as we played in the tidal pool, the world ceased to exist.

* * * * *

That Saturday, I saw Jessica walking back from the store. She had Tommy Hagen, her neighbor's four-year-old, in tow. The sun was just setting across the water, casting a warm glow the color of an orange traffic cone on the houses of the village.

Tom was tired and moved mechanically—kicking rocks along the middle of the road.

"Move it," she told him. She had often complained to me that two bucks an hour for baby-sitting wasn't worth it.

"I um," whined Tommy deeply. He was suffering from one of his numerous colds. He looked up at Jessica and gave a pathetic smile. She rolled her eyes, but bent down so he could climb up onto her back. When they turned down Shoreline she began to jog. Hanging on to her neck,

Tommy laughed and then covered her eyes with his pudgy hands.

"Hey!"

They spun and landed in a pile in front of my house.

"Huh, huh . . . huh, huh, huh," Tom laughed, his nose full.

That's when she noticed them—the two figures standing by the front window in my house. Two guys in dark suits. Familiar faces.

The missionaries were in my living room, standing in front of the fireplace just like they belonged, and Jessica was furious.

"Cum onnn," said Tom. He was standing a couple of yards away, flapping his arms up and down.

"Yeah, yeah." She pulled herself away from my window, and they trudged the last few meters home.

* * * * *

On Saturday nights, I would usually stop by Jessica's house and we'd wander together down to the town building where a movie was showing or a band would play. That night I knocked about seven, and Jessica was already ready. She had done her hair and was wearing a new, blue shirt open at the collar over a white T-shirt and looked pretty good. She grabbed her coat, and we dug our hands in our pockets and walked outside. Since it was too early to go to the movie, we headed down to the harbor.

The wind had been blowing in from the sea all day, and it was spraying a cold mist over the edge of town. But as we crunched along the gravel road, the wind began to die and the beginnings of a fog began rolling in from the ocean.

I was whistling between my teeth. I couldn't whistle

very well, and I only did it when I had something on my mind.

"You ever get sick? I mean really sick?" I asked her. It wasn't my real question, it was a warmup.

"You ever see me go to the hospital?" She asked me back.

"I guess not."

"Then you know the answer."

We walked a little more before I said, "I was just thinking, I could be a doctor one day."

"I guess. I can see you cutting people up, taking out stuff, charging them lots of money."

I laughed. "Yeah, I could do that."

We walked a bit more, thinking about Dr. Ian, until I said, "I guess you saw those Mormon guys were over today, huh?"

"Humph."

I took a glance at her, to size up her mood, then added, "They said your mom sent them."

I noticed her face redden. "My *mom* sent 'em?"

"That's what they said."

"I'm gonna . . . Geez, I'm sorry."

I shrugged. "I don't care. Doesn't bug me."

We rounded the fence at the bottom of Shoreline and jumped the rough edge at the head of the dock, taking two boards with every step. Farther along we walked into the cold ocean fog that hung like a veil. We were alone. No one came out on the dock at night.

"They want to come back again," I told her.

"They always do," Jessica said. "That's their job: to come back and back until you join."

"Join what?"

"The Church. The Mormon Church."

"Nah, they didn't say that," I said. "They were just visiting."

She laughed. "Sanchez is from the states. You think he came to Wolf Point to talk hockey with your dad?"

I shrugged.

"They give you a lesson?" she asked.

"I guess. They talked a lot."

"They teach you how to pray?"

"Yeah."

"That's the first discussion. They want you to join," she said.

"Hmmm."

We reached the end of the pier and leaned on the rail—the same rail that one winter I had licked to see if my tongue would really stick to frozen metal. It did. And for a month I had talked with a lisp.

We stared out at the water, but it was too dark and the fog was too thick to see much.

"Okay, I got a question," I said, nodding my head.

"Always."

I ignored her jab and said, "The Mormon guys said the Book of Mormon is just like the Bible. I know that's not right cause it says at the end of the Bible that there isn't supposed to be anything added to the Bible."

"Well . . . umm . . . I learned about that in Sunday School once, but I don't remember the answer."

"And they told us about the guy who said he saw God and started the Mormons."

"Joseph Smith."

"Yeah, I'd always thought it was Brigham Young, but they said it was Smith. Anyway, how does anybody know he didn't just write the book himself?"

"Well, there were a bunch of witnesses who saw the plates he translated it from," she said.

"Yeah, they were probably Mormons too. Do you guys pray to him, like Catholics pray to Mary?"

I kept asking questions, most of which Jess couldn't answer. Finally she drew in a breath, ready to say something, but stopped.

"What?" I asked.

"Nothing."

"You can't do that. What?"

"All right, I was just thinking that I'm sick of defending the Church. Most of the time it's just embarrassing to be a Mormon." She opened her mouth again, but stopped. She took a second and then asked, "Can I be alone for awhile?"

"Okay . . . I guess."

I walked along the pier and Jessica sat down on the edge and looked out into the harbor. Out in the night the dim lights of a trawler at anchor bobbed in and out of view in the fog. High bells echoed slowly from the channel buoys—a long, round tone. It was a pretty, haunting sound.

After five minutes the cold was inching through my sweater. After ten minutes I was ready to go, but she was still lost in thought. It took her fifteen to eventually get up and walk over to me.

"Thanks," she said.

"No problem," I said, rubbing my hands together. "You gonna tell me what you were thinking?"

"I wasn't thinking anything."

"Yes, you were."

"I'm serious. I was praying," she said.

"Oh." I didn't know what to say to that.

She leaned against the rail with me. "I know it's weird. I just got a feeling to pray. I don't know why."

"So what'd you pray about?"

"You."

I smiled. "Little old me?"

"Wise guy. Yes, you. I told Heavenly Father that I didn't know if the Church was true or not, and if He didn't mind I was going to go ahead and tell you that."

"And?"

"He didn't answer."

"Huh?" I said.

"Or maybe He did, I don't know. I got a feeling I should tell you something—something I heard at church once."

"Okay. I'm listening."

"Well, this old guy told a story about a kid who was eighteen and went to work on a fishing boat out of St. John's. And sometime in the summer of his first year on the boat it hit a sandbar and was sunk. Most of the crew climbed aboard the lifeboat, but this guy and the captain got caught by the current and dragged away."

"They didn't have life jackets or anything, and for a long time they just treaded water—hoping for someone to find 'em."

"Wow," I said. I'd been on enough fishing boats to know how big the ocean was, and how impossible it would be to find anyone swimming in it.

"Anyway, finally the captain realizes that the water's too cold for them to last much longer, so he swims over to the kid and says, 'We ain't gonna make it.' And he asks the kid if he's religious. Well, the kid is just like me. He's a Mormon, but he's been kind of goofing off, and it's been a while since he's been active. But since he's a goner, he says he'll say a prayer for 'em."

67

"And what happened?"

"He and the captain closed their eyes and the kid says a prayer out loud . . . and when they open their eyes they see the light of a buoy. They swim over and hang on and a few hours later they were found."

I smiled. "And the guy telling the story at church turns out to be the eighteen-year-old kid, right?"

"Uh, no. The guy telling the story was the captain. He joined the Church."

"Hmm."

Jessica stood up straight and put her hands in her pockets, but then she took them out and leaned against the rail again. Maybe she was feeling guilty for not being able to answer all my questions, or maybe she just felt awkward because we had never talked about religion and she wasn't really sure what to say next.

"I don't know why that story came to me," she said.

I didn't make a guess.

"You said the missionaries told you how to pray. Did they say a prayer too?" she asked.

"Yeah, but no one was drowning."

"Wise guy. How did it make you feel?"

"I don't know, didn't think about it." I looked out to the ocean and breathed out. "Okay, maybe I thought about it."

She turned to me, her eyes wide. "And?"

I let out a snicker. "Before I left tonight I prayed by myself."

She smiled and reached up and put her hand on my shoulder.

"That's pretty cool."

"Thanks." I didn't turn or move because I liked the

68

touch of her hand on my shoulder. How strange, I thought.

"You know, you're the best friend I've ever had," she said.

"I'm the *only* friend you've ever had," I replied.

8

THE TRIP TO BALLYCATER

Early on Monday morning, I was awakened by a pounding on my back door. It was Jess, and before I had a chance to ask why she was waking me at six o'clock on one of the last days of summer, she said, "Lights."

I looked outside. The sun was just breaking over the island, casting long, red shadows onto the water. Though it was early, the fishing fleet was already at sea, except for one late-departing trawler that was steaming out of the harbor, leaving a white wake in the ocean and a boiling cloud of inky diesel exhaust in the clear sky.

I combed my matted hair with my fingers and squinted at her. "What?"

"We need light. On the water. To find our way in and out of Ballycater. I saw the lights on the trawler on Saturday night, but it didn't click until this morning. But it would work. We can lay out a pathway of floating lights."

I rubbed the sleep out of my eyes and shook my head. "Who are you?"

"Just get dressed."

"Are you lost? Do you live around here?"

"Hurry up. We've got work to do."

I obeyed and went back to my room to change into jeans and my favorite University of Wolf Point sweatshirt that I'd bought at Chern's store.

"I'm having some toast," I said, walking back into the kitchen where Jess was waiting. "Breakfast is the most important meal of the day."

"Just hurry," Jess said.

I pulled out our glass-covered butter dish and a loaf of bread and stuffed a couple of slices into the toaster. "Well, I can't hurry the toasting process. You can't hurry science. . . . You want a piece?"

"Maybe."

I buttered the toast and we sat at our blue kitchen table. Jessica was lost in thought. She looked tired, and while we were eating, I asked, "Were you up late last night?"

"Why?" she said, all defensive.

"I don't know. Your eyes look tired."

When we were younger, I never worried about what I said to Jess. But in the last year or so, it was hard to know how she was going to react. Now, I thought she was going to jump at me. But after a moment she said, "Yeah, I was."

"So what were you doing?" I asked.

As soon as I said it, I wished I hadn't. It was the type of question that would set her off. But she answered me quietly.

"Reading."

"Reading what?"

She didn't answer right away. Instead, she took another bite of toast.

"Don't laugh," she warned.

I shrugged, a "what could I have to laugh about" shrug. She continued, "I couldn't sleep and was looking for something to read when I found my old Book of Mormon. You know, I've got red and yellow highlighter on just about every page, but I realized I had no idea of what was in there. I ended up reading most of the night."

I waited for her to explain more, but instead, her mood changed. She stood up and stepped to the sink where she filled a glass with water. By the time she turned back to me, her eyes were clear and she was all business again. We turned our attention to her plan to tame Ballycater, deciding we'd need a dozen or more floating lights with some sort of anchor for each. And we'd need a fish sonar to gauge the depth, and a couple of strong poles to allow us to move among the rocks.

"We need more help," I suggested. "We need a couple of strong bodies on the poles."

"Maybe Megan?" asked Jessica, but we both shook our heads.

"Would your dad do it?" she asked.

"He's inland. But even if he were here he wouldn't. No adult's gonna do it. They know about Ballycater. We need a couple of saps who've never heard of the cove."

And at that moment we both knew who fit the bill.

* * * * *

"We were going up to Derwin Gray's lighthouse today," said Elder Sanchez on Chern's front step. "He's coming in his boat to pick us up at noon. He said we could give him and his wife a couple of lessons."

"Perfect," I said. "The cove . . . ur, the place we're going is on the way to North Point. We could take you on from there. It'd save him a couple of trips in his boat."

"You'd be doing us a big favor. And you could talk to both of us about the Church," added Jessica. "You guys can ride in boats, can't you?"

"Sure," said Sanchez, "our mission president gave us permission to ride in boats while we're in Wolf Point because, well, you folks don't have any other way to get around."

"It'd be a good chance to get us alone for a couple of hours," said Jessica.

It was obvious they both knew we had another motive for inviting them, but that went unsaid.

"Come on," said Jessica. "We don't have all day to wait. We'll just go without you."

The two missionaries looked worried about that and whispered to each other.

"We don't want you to go off alone," said Elder Shackelford. "But we'd need to make sure it's okay with your parents."

"They don't care," I added.

"Well, just to be safe, I think it best if we pay both moms a visit."

"Whatever."

* * * * *

While we waited for the two elders to return, I took another chance with Jess.

"You know, . . . I've been wondering about something," I said to her.

"Oh, yeah?"

"I don't want to upset you or anything, but I'd kind of like to know."

She nodded, turning serious.

"It's a tough question. You may not like it."

"Will you just ask me?"

74

I let out a big breath. "All right. I'd kind of like to know what we're looking for now. I mean, do you think your dad's . . . um . . . do you think he's alive in there, in the cove?"

She turned pale. "I don't know. I haven't wanted to think about that."

"Sorry."

"No, that's okay. I mean, it's crazy to think we'll find him in there. It's been weeks." Her eyes got moist and her voice cracked, but she held back any tears. "I guess part of me still hopes we'll find him alive. But the realistic side needs to find his wreckage to prove that he's not . . . not coming back. Just to settle things for me, and so that Mom can get the insurance money."

"I'm sorry I asked. I was just curious."

"No, it's okay. You have a right to know."

* * * * *

After another fifteen minutes or so, Sanchez and Shackelford arrived at the boat, still wearing their suits and walking shoes.

"Why aren't you ready?" I asked.

"We are. Your moms said we could take a ride."

"But you didn't change."

"Why would we change?"

"You guys are weird."

"You don't know the half of it," Elder Shackelford said.

The missionaries and Jess stepped into the boat, and I pushed us off the beach. With a one-hop splash I jumped into the stern and pulled the motor to life. I set the throttle to full and the boat edged out of harbor and around the coast. A lone seal was sitting on the harbor buoy, and he watched the boat as it passed—weighed heavy with Jess and me and a pair of guys in dark suits.

75

When we were out in the fishing lane, Shackelford shifted his long legs among the cargo. The bottom was littered with a pile of gas lamps, a long coil of rope, a couple of rolls of duct tape, and an odd collection of floating devices—from kids' swimming rings to innertubes.

"What's with all the lamps and other stuff?" he asked, lifting the frayed end of a rope with one of his well-worn, black mailman shoes.

"We may hit some fog," said Jessica, who didn't turn from her perch in the front of the boat.

We plowed along at a steady pace for half an hour as the missionaries and I exchanged small talk and they answered my questions about the States and Montreal. Then Sanchez pulled out his scriptures and began reading silently. Shackelford dutifully followed his senior companion's lead.

"You guys reading the Book of Mormon?" I asked.

Shackelford shook his head. "I've actually been reading the Old Testament. It's a rush."

"Yeah, right."

"It is . . . really. You ever read much of the Bible?"

"'In the beginning' . . . I never got past that."

Shackelford grinned.

"I'm gonna wait for the movie," I added, and laughed at my own joke.

"I've heard that one before," said Sanchez, his eyes still moving across the page. "But there's wisdom in these pages, and you'd never get that from Hollywood." He looked up at me and added: "They'd probably cast Tom Cruise as Moses."

Jessica turned to the missionaries. She watched them reading for a moment, then let out a sigh. "All right," she said, "Ian wants to know some stuff about the Book of Mormon."

"Hmmm," from Sanchez.

"What did you want to know?" she asked, but I shrugged. I'd had a thousand other questions on my mind since then. "He wanted to know about something in the Bible that says there wouldn't be any other scriptures," said Jessica.

"Of course," said Sanchez, turning to face me. "We get asked that a lot. There is a reference in the Book of Revelation that, we believe, is referring to that particular book—not to the entire Bible."

"That's kind of convenient, isn't it?" asked Jessica. "You twist things in there to fit what you want it to."

"You know, it's like anything in the Bible, or the Book of Mormon, or any of the scriptures—you have to find out for yourself if its true by praying and studying," said Sanchez. "It's true, the message we share requires faith—"

"But it all fits together," Elder Shackelford added. "I joined the Church when I was a couple of years younger than you. But I didn't believe it all at first. Even when I finally prayed about it, and I got the feeling that it was right, that didn't mean I believed everything the missionaries had to say or that was taught in church. In fact, I didn't believe most of it at first. But I still joined. I still got baptized."

"Why would you do that?" I asked.

"Because . . . I don't know, I guess I knew it was the right place to be. I guess I felt that I would believe more and more pieces eventually. And I did, even though I still have questions and doubts, even today when I'm on a mission. I guess that's why I envy people like Jess who've had the Church all their lives."

She laughed. "No. Converts have it better."

"Not from where I sit. I always thought that if I'd been a member all my life, I'd have less doubts. You know, I wasn't even sure there was a God before I joined the Church. You always grew up with that as a given."

She thought for a minute. "I guess I never thought of it that way. But you never grew up being the only Mormon in your school or in your town. It's embarrassing."

"You'd be surprised," Elder Shackelford said. "I lost a lot of friends when I joined the Church."

They stopped talking for a minute, probably when they all realized I was listening.

"I guess this isn't the best thing to be talking about in front of someone who's only had one lesson," said Shackelford, looking at Sanchez for support.

"Probably not," Sanchez agreed. "Ian, do you have any questions about Mormons?"

"He's always got questions," said Jess.

I wrinkled my nose at her and thought for a moment. "I guess." But I didn't continue.

"Well?" Jess finally asked.

I looked up at her and then at the missionaries. "Well, I guess I'd want to know where people go . . . when they die," I said quietly. They all knew I was talking about Jess's dad.

"That's a good question," said Sanchez. "Christ explained the heavens in his ministry on earth. He said people can live in several degrees of glory, depending upon their worthiness on the earth. We don't believe in the traditional heaven and hell that many religions do, but in a loving God who has made a way for us to live with him and our family members forever."

"That why Jess's mom has that 'Families Are Forever' knitting thing hanging on her wall?" I asked.

"It's needlework," said Jess.

"Yeah. One thing that sets Mormons apart from other religions is our belief in families being together in the afterlife," Sanchez explained.

"Jess's dad isn't a Mormon. Does that matter?" I asked.

The group was quiet for a second.

"We can do baptisms for nonmembers who . . . um . . . die before they join the Church," said Sanchez.

"Of course," Shackelford added quickly, "we hope that Jess's dad is alive and well."

"That's pretty cool, I guess," I added, "that you can be with your family forever."

Then we saw the dark outline of rocks edging Ballycater Cove.

The two elders turned and looked at each other with such alarm that a chill went down my spine.

"Where are we going?" Sanchez asked us.

Jessica didn't turn from her position in the front of the boat. "To a cove."

"Can we stop the boat?" Sanchez asked.

"Why?" I asked.

"Please."

I killed the motor and the boat settled into the waves. Jessica turned to face the missionaries and the four of us sat in a circle in my tiny fishing boat as Sanchez carefully zipped his scriptures into their leather case.

"We didn't have a prayer," said Sanchez. "And I think we need one."

Jess and I looked at each other then at our feet. I just hoped he didn't make me say it.

"Elder Shackelford, would you ask it?" said Sanchez.

"Sure."

We bowed our heads and Elder Shackelford offered up a short prayer, asking for safety and guidance. He finished and looked at me. "Now where are you taking us? I have a bad feeling, and we're not supposed to ignore these things."

I let out a large breath, an attempt at frustration, but in reality I was a little amazed at the missionaries' perception. It was too weird.

"We told you, we're heading to a cove—Ballycater Cove," I said.

"What's so special about the cove?" Shackelford asked.

"It's pretty foggy. And there's a lot of rocks."

"So it's dangerous?" Sanchez said.

Silence.

"So why are we going?" he asked.

I looked at Jess, but she was still looking at the bottom of the boat as she rocked her foot back and forth.

"She thinks her dad's in there," I added. "She thinks he spoke to her."

"Shut up!" Jess snapped. "I never said you could tell anyone."

"You never said I couldn't. And I figure they should know."

Jess stared out into the ocean. Sanchez spoke next.

"I don't really know what to think," he said quietly. "But something *has* happened around here. I feel something, and I think Elder Shackelford does too."

Shackelford nodded. "Something has happened here."

9

THE DISCOVERY

Jess set the first lantern in the water at the head of the cove. In the daylight it seemed small and pathetic floating on the huge ocean.

"There's no fog now, but it comes in fast," I told the missionaries.

Jess set a new light every hundred yards or so, dropping her makeshift anchors into the swirling water to hold the lanterns in place.

The two missionaries were kneeling in the front of the boat, each holding an oar like a javelin, intently staring into the dark-green water.

"What happens if I miss a rock?" asked Sanchez.

"We get wet . . . very wet," said Shackelford.

"Just don't miss," I said.

Placing the lanterns was slow work, and it took until noon to crawl halfway into the cove.

"My knees are killing me," said Sanchez.

"We can't stop," I told him. "We don't want to get caught in here."

"Missionaries should develop strong knees," said Shackelford. "It's good for praying."

We passed an ominous black rock as large and square

as a school bus on end. I met Jess's gaze briefly. It was the same rock we had almost run into in the fog. I could see her shiver with the memory.

"There are hidden rocks around here," I said to the missionaries. "Just under the water." I let off on the throttle and the boat slowed to a crawl. Elder Shackelford put his oar into the water and guided us around a jagged rock hidden just below the waterline.

We went another fifty yards and Jess pushed the remaining light off and announced, "I'm out of lanterns." We all lifted netting and looked under the seats and nodded.

"Will that be enough?" Sanchez asked.

"It'll have to be," said Shackelford.

We cleared the shadow of the rock, and I warmed the engine back up. Still no fog on the horizon. The land was clear about a mile ahead—a rocky, forbidding place with the single patch of green that I steered for. We all watched the land intently as the blowing crabgrass slowly came into focus. On the slope, a few wild crocuses were growing out of the poor soil. They were blue and yellow and moving gently—out of place in the horrible cove.

We reached shore and Elder Shackelford jumped out first. With an effortless pull he lifted the heavy front end of the boat out of the water and dragged the entire boat and crew up the steep shore. Jess and I climbed out next, but Elder Sanchez was looking out to sea. He was transfixed, watching something.

We all turned and saw it. Jess brought her hand to her mouth and held her breath. I stood quiet, feeling the heavy beating of my heart. A silent gray fog was rolling around the north point of the cove.

Elder Shackelford was not intimidated. He raised his

eyebrows and broke the silence. "We'd probably better get moving," he said. "Let's do whatever it was we came here to do."

Jess nodded. "I guess we're looking for wreckage," she said.

We split up. The elders scrambled over living-room sized rocks in their suits and dress shoes while Jess and I moved south along the grassy shoreline that quickly turned into a field of brown rocks.

Now and then we would look out to sea. The mist was slowly filling the cove, sending out long, white fingers over the water and then filling in behind until all was lost in fog the color of a thundercloud. Then the fog started coming from the east, from somewhere inland, cold and wet and enveloping.

As we picked our way through the rocks, I tried not to think about the heavy silence of the cove, about the voice that could, at any moment, haunt my best friend. After awhile Jessica climbed onto a large boulder for a wider view of the terrain. She had just reached the top when the quiet was broken by a rough splash as the ocean broke against the rocks. She jumped slightly, uncharacteristically.

"There's something down there," she said to me.

I looked up at her. She was just visible in the gathering fog, but I could see her hair was wet from the spray of the wave. She was pointing toward the ocean.

Jessica jumped down from her perch. It was too high, and she slipped on the wet rock and landed on one knee on the granite surface. She winced with the pain, but I pulled her up, and in a second she'd found her footing, and we made our way to the water. We straddled a crag of rock and looked down into a small pool. In the half-light it was hard to make out shapes and colors, but it slowly came clear—a dirty collection of rigging and dark wood, being washed in the surging surf.

I looked out to sea, watching for the approach of the next wave, but seeing nothing, quickly lowered myself into the rock crag and fished something out of the cold water. I held it up for Jess to see. It was a piece of green wood, about a foot long. A piece of the hull of a boat.

It was part of her father's boat.

"Oh," said Jess. There was a sad relaxation throughout her body, like she had just let out a huge breath of air.

"Oh," she said again, and sat down hard on the closest rock.

I scrambled out and dropped the piece of wood on the ground. Quietly I sat down next to Jess and felt for her hand and grabbed it. She held on tight and then crowded against me. I put my arm around her as she began to cry. It was the first time I'd ever felt that Jessica needed me. I didn't know what to say, so I just sat there next to her without speaking.

She caught her breath, but couldn't hold it back. The emotions she had kept bottled up were suddenly released, as if a dam had burst. For five minutes we sat together like that, with the realization that the search was over.

"We found something." It was one of the missionaries calling. The voice broke us out of our trance.

"Okay," I called. I stood up, then bent down to pick up the piece of wood. Taking Jessica's hand, I led her back toward the boat. She moved like a ghost, her face as white as bone, her shoulders drooping, her eyes as dead as the brown rocks under our feet.

"We . . . um . . . we found something," Elder Shackelford said, his head bent down.

"We did too," I said. I nodded at the ghost beside me, and they realized she knew.

Shackelford stepped forward and handed Jess a watertight box. "We found this in the water, lodged in the rocks."

She looked at the box sadly. "It's Dad's log," she said, wiping a tear off her face. After a moment, she added, "Thanks."

* * * * *

Jessica and I stepped into the boat. Sanchez looked at the foggy sea and then back at the tiny fishing boat. "Couldn't we walk?" he asked. He was serious.

"Take you about a week," I told him.

Sanchez looked out to sea again and then at his companion.

"Just like riding in a car, Elder," said Shackelford, pushing him in.

Without another word the big elder pushed us off. I pulled the outboard, but nothing happened. I pulled again, but it wouldn't catch in the damp air. I pulled a dozen times before pausing to catch my breath. My boat was moving farther out into the cove, deeper into the fog. The waves had picked up and the boat was beginning to lift high on each crest.

"It's never done this," I said, nodding toward the outboard. Sanchez was clearly worried.

"We'd better get back to shore," said Shackelford.

We looked around but realized we'd lost sight of land.

"Land is east," I said, holding my compass close. I squinted to see the land but shook my head. "I don't think we should try it."

"Why?" asked Sanchez.

"Too many rocks," said Shackelford. "Let's try and get out of the cove. We'll row."

Sanchez held his breath and we began picking our way carefully out to sea. Before we'd traveled a hundred yards we hit the heavy fog.

"Watch for our first light," I said.

High above a seagull screamed and I shivered. I tried the outboard again, but no luck. There was no wind, and the fog had set in. The eerie mist was so thick I could barely see the missionaries rowing in the bow. And still, the boat was climbing and falling heavily on the waves that were over three feet and building. Soon the swells were whitecapping and crashing into the boat from every direction. We were taking on water.

"Um, it's pretty bad," I told them, an immense under-statement.

"I can't see the end of my oar," said Elder Sanchez.

"Just keep your rowing steady," Elder Shackelford said calmly. "We're not in a rush."

"Yeah, but it could get worse," I said.

"It could get worse?" Sanchez asked.

"Oh, yeah. When you can't see your hand in front of your face we'd better stop."

"I don't want to stop," said Jessica, her head was between her knees as she sat in the wet bottom of the boat.

"I'm glad we said a prayer," said Shackelford.

"Me too," said Elder Sanchez.

"Me too," I said.

Just then the boat was thrown down the side of a six-foot wave, the biggest yet. We held on as the boat crashed into the water on the other side. There was no relief.

Again, another wave picked up the boat. We were all sloshing about in the water that was rising in the bottom.

"We're going to drown," Sanchez muttered under his breath. He'd given up rowing. But as the boat reached the top of the next wave he straightened. "I see a lantern," he yelled, as we went sliding down the back end of the swell. "I think," he added.

"Yeah, I saw it," I said, pointing toward a yellow light that was just growing visible in the distance.

"How did it get so . . . ? . . . that's not . . ."

The light was too high, and was moving on the waves. Shackelford stopped rowing, and we all realized there was another sound in the cove, very near, growing louder and louder until it became a deafening, groaning noise that filled the sodden air.

All four bodies lowered until just our heads peered out of the boat—like young birds in a floating nest. Jessica and I were about to meet the fabled demon boat that drowned fools who ventured into Ballycater. The elders probably didn't know what to think. They just remained glued to the soggy bottom of the boat with their mouths agape.

Then without warning the noise stopped and a blinding light swept over my small boat. Sanchez dropped his oar into the water, said "Oh," and splashed around in the salt water to fish it out—soaking the arm of his suit to the shoulder. Eventually he gave up. The oar was lost in the mountainous waves.

"Ahoy, on the boat," came a booming voice. "This is the *Halifax*."

The missionaries looked at each other, confused.

"It's the Coast Guard," said Jessica, and we all began breathing again.

"Come about and we can take you on," said the booming megaphone voice.

"Try and stop us," said Sanchez as he stood up and waved at the light, rocking the small boat dangerously.

The *Halifax* came into view and the crew dropped a rope ladder. Jess went up first and then the missionaries followed. I went last, tying my boat to a drag line.

With sonar and a strong hull, the boat maneuvered out of the cove easily—only stopping every now and then to fish Jessica's lanterns out of the water. The crew was busy and ignored us until we were clear of the fog and the big waves and out on the open sea. Finally, a young, blond sailor climbed down from the bridge.

"I'm Claude Monteau, first mate," he said, shaking all our hands. "Good thing I spotted your lights." He had a thick, French Canadian accent and seemed pleased with himself for the rescue.

"Yeah, thanks," I said. "We could have been fish bait—"

I caught myself and looked at Jessica, but she was leaning against the rail, lost in thought.

"We found some wreckage in the cove," Elder Shackelford said to the mate. "And a ship's log."

The man looked doubtful. He glanced around our group and stopped on the two elders. He obviously did not see guys dressed in suits out on the ocean very often. He looked all of us over once again and shook his head. "Well, let's go see the captain and file a report."

Jessica stepped in front of him and handed the watertight box over. The mate took it gingerly.

"It's from my dad's boat," she said, a tear frozen on her cheek. For the first time in my life Jessica looked vulnerable and small to me.

"Oh," said the mate.

"He went missing about a month ago," I added.

"Right . . . I remember."

* * * * *

The cruiser moved slowly south, cutting through waves in a steady jump that lulled us into a trance as we sat on the deck.

Finally Elder Shackelford lifted his head up. "I'm sorry I never got to meet your dad," he said to Jessica.

For a second her eyes flickered with life. She smiled thinly and nodded her head. "You'd have liked him."

"What was he like?"

She shrugged. "I don't know. He was pretty funny, I guess. He knew every joke ever told and every song. . . . Nobody knew it, but he used to sing on his boat."

"It's true," I said. "I was out on the north beach once and the wind was carrying inland and I heard him. It was awful."

We all laughed.

"And he let me steer his boat," I added. "I don't know anyone else who would trust a goofy kid to steer his boat. He was pretty cool."

"Teaching responsibility was his big thing." said Jessica.

We hadn't moved by the time the Coast Guard reached Wolf Point. By then, it was well past midday and the sun was still high over the ocean but arching to the west. The boat's nose turned and followed its own shadow to the village tucked into the back of the bay.

At that point all our minds were on Jessica's father. I imagined Jessica was thinking that he'd never again make the turn out of the fishing channel into the bay, that he'd never see the blue and yellow houses on the hill and follow Shoreline up to the end and pick out his own, that he'd never see the white smoke rising out of his chimney and know that dinner was on.

"Wherever you are, Dad," Jessica said quietly, "wherever you go, I will remember you. I will do something for you."

And she did.

10

ANOTHER VOICE

It was five o'clock in the morning when Elders Shackelford and Reed climbed on the bus. The road was wet but clear, and the houses and buildings they passed were all dark and quiet. Eddy stuffed his hands deep into his coat pockets and blew a breath of steam onto the window. He was thinking of home again. He couldn't help himself. In less than a month he'd climb on another bus to Montreal.

The bus stopped on the east side of the city and Elders Gaston and Schumann climbed aboard and slid into the seats in front of them.

"Morning, boys," said Gaston.

"Ugh," from Eddy.

This was Eddy's fourth visit to Toronto in two years, and the bus ride seemed longer each time. The Toronto temple was the nearest to the Newfoundland mission, and the missionaries and their mission president made this trip in a large group twice a year. Gaston was green. Like a puppy, he was excited just to be going somewhere in a vehicle.

The bus pulled away from the last St. John's stop and picked up speed as it wound its way through the heart of

Newfoundland. Gradually dawn broke behind them and lit up the landscape and burned the frost from the cool fall morning. Eddy leaned his shoulder against the dirty pane and watched the power lines dip and rise and studied the occasional stone farmhouse that slid by. This part of the world was a strange place, Eddy thought for the thousandth time. A place of rocks and moss and rabbits. A desolate spot, but remarkable, even beautiful.

"You know, I'll miss it here," Eddy said to his companion.

Reed perked up and nodded like a fool. "Yeah, me too." Reed still had a year and a half left, but was eager to please his seasoned senior companion.

The bus settled into a steady rocking motion through the wide open terrain and Eddy closed his eyes and slumped into his seat. In a minute he was asleep and didn't wake until the stop in Gander.

At two o'clock they boarded the ferry to Nova Scotia. It was a weekend, and inside, the boat was crowded and stuffy, warm with red-faced islanders and tourists in wind breakers making the run to the mainland. The missionaries found a booth tucked in the back of the ferry's onboard restaurant and ate all-you-can-eat tomato soup and crackers until they couldn't take another bite.

Finally Schumann pushed his fourth bowl away and looked at Elder Shackelford. "Well, short-timer, what's the first thing you're going to do when you get home?"

The others grinned like schoolboys.

The big hockey player smiled and shook his head. "Haven't thought about it," he lied.

"Yeah, right."

"Well, it would feel good to pull on a pair of skates again."

"B-o-r-r-ing," said Gaston. "The first thing I'm gonna do is kiss a girl. Any girl. She could even be ugly. I don't care."

They all laughed.

"Hockey's my priority, I guess," said Eddy. "I was dating a girl when I left, but I haven't heard from her in a while. She's probably married by now."

"Or fat," said Schumann. "Myself, I broke up with every girl I knew before I left—even those I never dated." The elders laughed again.

"I'm serious," Schumann continued. "I had a big speech worked out and gave it to every one of them. And you know what? All those girls thought I was really righteous for not wanting to think about them on my mission. And, subconsciously, I think that they didn't like being dumped and wanted to get me back."

"Sure," said Gaston.

"It's true," Schumann added. "Every one of them has written to me." He tapped the side of his head to indicate superior intelligence.

Eddy rolled his eyes. "They just feel sorry for you."

"Ahhh."

"So you're a hockey player?" Gaston asked Eddy.

Eddy shrugged. "Used to be. We'll see when I get home if I can still play. It's been a while."

"Didn't your stake president say that you'd come home a better hockey player?" asked Schumann, smiling.

Eddy guffawed. "No. He told me the truth. He said I'd come back overweight and slow. I sure didn't come to Newfoundland to become a better hockey player. . . . I knew it'd be a sacrifice."

"All good things are," said Schumann, turning serious for once.

Eddy nodded. "Yes, they are."

It was late the next afternoon when the bus climbed a small rise just out of Oshawa and the missionaries spotted the distinctive CNN Tower and the downtown Toronto skyline. Eddy warmed to the sight. Gaston and Schumann, half hysterical with excitement after the long journey, stood up and began singing loudly, "Come, Come, Ye Saints."

Eddy let them sing a full verse and chorus before reaching up and pushing their heads down. "You wanna get us kicked off the bus?" he asked. He stuffed them back into their seats with such little effort that they shut up as demanded.

Still, even their silly behavior couldn't dampen Eddy's spirits. It'd been a while since he'd been to the temple and he was excited about spending a few days working inside. The temple was much like Newfoundland, he thought. It was a place that was at the same time strange and remarkable.

"The Lord has walked these halls," a temple worker had told him on his first visit, and Eddy had nodded and believed him. That day he had felt the Spirit so strong that his legs weakened. Since the Toronto temple was almost a thousand miles away, he and his fellow missionaries had only been allowed back a couple of times since then. But with each visit the Spirit returned and the place seemed a little less strange and more like a second home—just much cleaner and whiter.

He saw her on the last day of their visit.

Eddy and his companion had just finished their second full temple session of the day and were walking in a group down a long hallway toward the cafeteria when Eddy glanced into the baptismal room. There was a group

94

of high-school-aged kids and a few parents all wearing white and standing in a line to do baptisms for the dead—an ordinance where the living stand in for relatives or strangers who were not baptized into the Church during their lifetimes.

Eddy surveyed the group, not sure what he was looking for. They looked the same as every other group he'd seen that week, but something told him they were different.

Then he saw her.

Jessica was standing next in line to go into the water. Her hands were on her hips and her jaw was clenched as she stood impatiently waiting her turn. *Just like Jessica,* thought Eddy, *mad that things aren't running faster.*

Jessica looked up just then and saw the familiar face in the doorway. It'd been almost a year since she'd seen his tall figure, and she looked surprised. She waved and smiled and then was beckoned into the warm water. As she descended the stairs into the font, Eddy noticed Brother Hagen, her neighbor from Wolf Point, standing behind her. He waved at Eddy, and then it was Brother Hagen's turn.

Eddy couldn't see into the font from where he stood, but he could see Hagen's weathered face and graying hair. And he heard the name spoken clearly: "Colin James O'Brien" and then the familiar words of the baptismal ordinance. He saw Brother Hagen's weathered face disappear and then pop back up a moment later, his dark hair dripping wet.

Eddy smiled. It was done. Jessica had gone to church and become worthy, traveled a thousand miles, and had done something for her father that he couldn't do for himself. She had brought someone to stand in his place in the baptismal waters.

"Lost something?" Elder Reed joined Eddy in the doorway.

"No," said Eddy. "You go on. I need to talk to someone."

"Grilled cheese for lunch. You'll miss out."

"I'll get over it."

After a while Jessica emerged from the lockers, wearing wet hair and dry clothes. Eddy extended his hand, but Jess stepped forward and gave him a hug. Then they both blushed.

"You here with Sanchez?" asked Jessica.

Eddy shook his head. "He's home in Texas now. Eating barbecued Iguana or whatever it is they do there."

She led Eddy to a row of velvet-covered benches and they sat. "You're about due to go home too, right?"

"Next month. Twenty-three days, two hours, fifteen minutes . . ."

She smiled. "Montreal, right?"

"Yup . . . So how's your mom?"

"Still a fanatic. A walking, talking Molly Mormon doll."

"There are worse things to be."

"Yeah, I know. She's okay."

"Is she making ends meet? I can't imagine it's easy."

"They paid on Dad's insurance money. And Mom and I find work here and there. It's been okay."

"How's everyone else—Ian and his little sister?"

"Ian's okay. Megan will be so jealous I saw you. She had the biggest crush on you."

"She did not." Eddy blushed again and rubbed his cheek with his hand.

Jessica rolled her eyes. "Quit being so humble, I'm not

buying it Anyway, they're fine. Megan's going to church just about every week . . . maybe every week, I don't know. Ian had the lessons, and I think he believes, but he's never wanted to come to church."

"You ever ask him?"

"The new missionaries did. I don't know what his problem is."

Eddy paused. He had a feeling he knew the hangup, but wasn't sure how Jessica would take it. He took a breath and plowed on.

"I think you're his problem."

Her smile disappeared. "Excuse me?"

"I imagine he wants *you* to ask him to church. If I know Ian, he wants to share this new part of his life with you."

"What does it matter if I ask him or the missionaries ask him?"

"Because he's not in love with the missionaries."

Jessica sat still, her mouth open and her face in obvious shock.

"You *had* to know," Eddy said. She shook her head. For a moment her tomboy facade faded and she looked vulnerable. "Well, he might not know either . . . if the truth is known," Eddy added.

She stared at the carpet and wiggled her feet.

"I probably should keep my big mouth shut, huh?" he asked. "You guys are too young to fall in love anyway."

Jessica turned to him. "You can fall in love at any age," she said. "To be truthful, I guess I've been in love with Ian since we were tiny kids. He's the smartest, strongest . . . I don't know, he's just more fun than any guy I've ever known."

"And he needs the Church in his life," said Eddy. "He's probably just about to turn eighteen—"

"He just did."

"Right, and he's searching for something right now. I know I was when I was his age."

Neither said anything for a long pause. They watched the kids from Jessica's group file out of the lockers and mill about in the waiting room.

Finally Eddy broke the quiet.

"You still hate missionaries?" he asked, and she laughed.

"No . . . well, not as much."

"You going to church?"

"I'm here aren't I?"

"Yes you are. You must have had a change of heart about things . . . about the Church that is."

Jessica bit her lip coyly. "You helped. And Elder Sanchez. And Ian. I got to feeling guilty about his Church questions and started reading the scriptures and going to church and I guess it became a bad habit." She held her breath and looked down. "And I got to thinking about the voice I heard in the cove and on the pier. I know Dad wanted something from me. I think he wanted me to do this."

"I think he did too. I'm sure he was watching."

She shook her head. "I have something else to tell you."

Eddy tilted his head. "Oh, yeah?"

"He was here, today. I heard him again and I saw him. Just now."

"Who?"

"My dad. After I came out of the water—in the font. Brother Hagen stepped down into the water and he looked up at me, but it wasn't his face anymore—it was Dad's. . . . This time it was really him."

"He say anything?"

Jess smiled, realizing how absurd it sounded. "You'll think I'm nuts."

"No I won't." He said it so seriously she knew he would believe her.

"He said, 'You found me, Jess.'"

A shiver shot up Eddy's spine and they sat for a moment in silence as they let the thought sink in. When Eddy finally looked at her, his eyes were tearing.

"You did," he said. "You found him."

Jessica couldn't help it. She was smiling, but a tear ran down her face too.

A moment later Brother Hagen walked by and shook Eddy's hand and nodded for Jessica to join her group that had begun moving out. Jessica shook hands with Eddy as they said a quick good-bye, but when she got to the door, she ran back and threw her arms around him.

"My dad would have liked to meet you," she said.

"We'll meet," he said.

She ran out of the room lightly, and her skirt flew about her legs like a bell. Watching her go, Eddy couldn't help thinking that the world is a good place.

ABOUT THE AUTHOR

Adrian Gostick began his writing career running a small-town newspaper in British Columbia, Canada. He has worked as a writer and editor for the *New Era* and is a frequent contributor to the magazine.

A graduate of both Ricks College and Brigham Young University, Adrian holds an associate's degree in communications and a bachelor's degree in journalism. He is employed by First Security Corporation where he is Vice President and Manager of Public Relations and Communications.

Adrian was born in England, but moved with his family to Montreal, Quebec, when he was ten years old. After joining The Church of Jesus Christ of Latter-day Saints at age twenty, he moved to the United States to attend college.

He is the author of numerous short stories and two other novels: *Eddy and the Habs* and *Impressing Jeanette*.

Adrian is married to Jennifer Lynne Raby, and they reside with their son, Anthony, in Oakley, Utah.

Adrian Gostick welcomes your input. Send e-mail to agostic@fscnet.com.

WHAT THEY'RE SAYING ABOUT *EDDY AND THE HABS*

Eddy and the Habs is one of those unique books that boys will love reading and their parents will heartily approve of. Full of action that is far from predictable, the book hits teen readers, especially boys, where they live— in sports. Eddy is the kid down the street when you were young who you were so grateful would be your friend. But there's nothing goody-goody or phony about him. He grows into a young man who makes the right decisions in the face of some pretty persuasive alternatives.

Parents won't have any trouble getting their children, especially their sons, to read this book. Just leave it out where they will see it, and soon it will disappear into a bedroom or backpack. It's that irresistible.

JANET THOMAS, ASSISTANT MANAGING EDITOR, *NEW ERA* MAGAZINE.

Eddy and the Habs is quite unlike most novels written for LDS teenagers. One of the things I like best about this book is that it is not so overtly "Mormon" as to put off readers who aren't LDS. *Eddy* is more than a novel about ice hockey, though the hockey scenes are superb. The scenes I remember most are those that reveal Eddy's growing maturity as he learns to deal with friends who

103

turn into enemies and a new religion and the decision to go on a mission.

Eddy and the Habs is a wonderful coming-of-age story that is sure to appeal to teenage LDS and non-LDS readers, whether or not they like sports or ice hockey.

CHRIS CROW, PROFESSOR OF ENGLISH, BRIGHAM YOUNG UNIVERSITY.

What is appealing about *Eddy and the Habs* is the way Latter-day Saint values are openly addressed for the general public. The characters are all "real," with problems, anxieties, and relevant issues in their lives. It is going to be a pleasure to recommend this book to families within the Church but also for others who want good literature and quality reading.

MARILOU SORENSEN, ASSOCIATE PROFESSOR OF EDUCATION, UNIVERSITY OF UTAH. (REVIEWED IN THE *DESERET NEWS*, SALT LAKE CITY, UTAH, SEPTEMBER 1994.)